I Have No Mouth & I Must Scream

BOOKS BY HARLAN ELLISON

NOVELS

The Sound of a Scythe [1960]
Web of the City [1958]
Spider Kiss [1961]

SHORT NOVELS

Doomsman [1967]
Run for the Stars [1991]
All the Lies That Are My Life [1980]
Mefisto in Onyx [1993]

GRAPHIC NOVELS

Demon with a Glass Hand
(adaptation with Marshall Rogers) [1986]
Night and the Enemy
(adaptation with Ken Steacy) [1987]
Vic and Blood:
The Chronicles of a Boy and His Dog
(adaptation with Richard Corben) [1989]
Harlan Ellison's Dream Corridor [1996]
Vic and Blood: The Continuing
Adventures of a Boy and His Dog
(adaptation with Richard Corben) [2003]
Harlan Ellison's Dream
Corridor Volume Two [2007]

SHORT STORY COLLECTIONS

The Deadly Streets [1958]
Sex Gang (as Paul Merchant) [1959]
A Touch of Infinity [1960]
Children of the Streets [1961]
Gentleman Junkie and Other Stories
of the Hung-Up Generation [1961]
Ellison Wonderland [1962]
Paingod and Other Delusions [1965]
I Have No Mouth & I
Must Scream [1967]
From the Land of Fear [1967]
Love Ain't Nothing But
Sex Misspelled [1968]
The Beast That Shouted Love at
the Heart of the World [1969]
Over the Edge [1970]
De Helden Van De Highway
(Dutch publication only) [1973]
All the Sounds of Fear
(British publication only) [1973]
The Time of the Eye
(British publication only) [1974]
Approaching Oblivion [1974]
Deathbird Stories [1975]
No Doors, No Windows [1975]
Hoe Kan Ik Schreeuwen
Zonder Mond
(Dutch publication only) [1977]
Strange Wine [1978]
Shatterday [1980]
Stalking the Nightmare [1982]
Angry Candy [1988]
Ensamvärk
(Swedish publication only) [1992]
Jokes Without Punchlines [1995]
Bce 3bykn Ctpaxa (All
Fearful Sounds)
(unauthorized Russian publication only) [1997]
The Worlds of Harlan Ellison
(authorized Russian publication only) [1997]
Slippage [1997]
Koletis, Kes Kuulutas
Armastust Maalima Siidames
(Estonian publication only) [1999]
La Machine aux Yeux Bleus
(French publication only) [2001]
Troublemakers [2001]
Ptak Smierci (The Best
of Harlan Ellison)
(Polish publication only) [2003]

I Have No Mouth &
I Must Scream

Harlan Ellison®

OPEN ROAD

INTEGRATED MEDIA

NEW YORK

978-1-4976-4307-9

This edition published in 2014 by Open Road Integrated Media, Inc.
345 Hudson Street
New York, NY 10014
www.openroadmedia.com

for
STUART ROBINSON *and* MARTIN SHAPIRO
who
never thought they'd be between covers together
but
mutual friendships make strange bedfellows
and
so you'll have to settle for 10% between you

Special thanks for assistance in the preparation of this book are extended by the Author to Linda M. Steele, David G. Hartwell, Ann Elizabeth Groban and David Calkins, the last–named of whom was directly responsible for noticing that "Pretty Maggie Moneyeyes" had been rewritten without my permission by unnamed and unknown parties, many times since its first publication, and that *all* versions of that most particular favorite of my stories currently in print—including the version in DEATHBIRD STORIES—are invalid. For the first time in fifteen years, Maggie appears as she was originally intended.

Table of Contents

I Have No Mouth &
I Must Scream

ECHOES OF SCREAMS, 1983

Virtually every line of this collection of stories has been revised for this new publication. What I consider to be at least four of my best stories are included in this volume. Those four needed very little attention, a comma here, a semicolon there. The introduction and the foreword have not been altered. Ted Sturgeon's dear words were very important to me in 1967 when they were shining new and this collection became the instrument that propelled my work and my career forward. To alter those words, or to solicit a new introduction by someone else, would be to diminish the gift that Ted conferred on me. This book has been in print constantly for sixteen years. And I take no small pleasure and pride in its contents. Only this need be said: I have learned the difference between "lie" and "lay," Ted.

I lay the success of these stories in part at the feet of Sturgeon; and that ain't no lie, kiddo.

HARLAN ELLISON
14 April 1983
Los Angeles

INTRODUCTION

THE MOVER, THE SHAKER

My report on Harlan Ellison's *Paingod* in *National Review* evoked the following, from a right–wing gentleman in Pennsylvania:

Harlan Ellison, contrary to the otherwise astute Theodore Sturgeon, is no more a major "prose stylist" than the editorial writer of the Plumber's Journal or *The New York Times*. Instead, he stands unchallenged as the god–awfullest writer ever to become submerged in the vaseline of synonyms and antonyms.

What Mr. Sturgeon mistakes for "image–making" is merely the slick conundrum of an empty–headed self–lover who, unhappily, believes that the bathroom ritual of personal daily resurrection, when inflated rhetorically, is 14" pegged prose. What emerges is not a "style" but rather a sort of neologistic bawling from the belly. It reminds one of the yips and yaps to be heard in the war councils of imbecilic demonstrators, from Berkley [sic] to Boston.

Ellison's "mad, mixed metaphors" are only less puerile than those of a certain Pennsylvania Supreme Court Justice, and his "unfinished sentences" no different in construction than those to be found in the diary of a lady golfer or political speech writer suffering from Liberal emphysema.

If our penitentiaries offered courses in creative writing we would soon be inundated with little Harlan Ellison's [the apostrophe also sic], all of them, to be sure, "groovy" and all of them ghastly. His unconcealed hostility toward his betters is evident in nearly everything he has ever written. That he is reviewed in a magazine noted for correct English (and often bad French) will probably embarrass the fellow. It does me.

To which I replied:

I find no hesitation in deeping Mr.— —'s embarrassment by demonstrating that he could not possibly have read my review of *Paingod and Other Delusions* with care, which leads inescapably to the deduction that he has not carefully read Ellison. For the tenor, sum and substance of my report was not that Harlan Ellison is a major prose stylist, but that in three to five years he shall be. Further, I did not in the review concede that Ellison is capable of atrociously bad writing—I proclaimed it. I said in effect that this extraordinarily energetic young writer is a man on the move, so watch him. Style, like taste, is resistant to lucid definition; however, both, as living things should be, are subject to constant change. For example, I can clearly recall the time when it was regarded as both stylish and tasteful to capitalize proprietary terms like Vaseline and God (at any degree of awfulness) and hardly tasteful to admit to any expertise on the style of ladies' diaries.

You hold in your hands a truly extraordinary book. Taken individually, each of these stories will afford you that easy–to–take, hard–to–find, *very* hard–to–accomplish quality of entertainment. Here are strange and lovely bits of bitterness like "Eyes of Dust" and the unforgettable "Pretty Maggie Moneyeyes," phantasmagoric fables like "I Have No Mouth & I Must Scream" and "Delusion for a Dragon Slayer."

I have something interesting to tell you about that last–mentioned story. Almost anyone who has been under the influence of a (and Purists please note: I tried) hallucinogen can recognize the "psychedelic" quality of this story and its images, even to a fine detail like the almost total absence of sound during the shipwreck sequence, and of course the kaleidoscopic changes of persona and symbol. Yet I know for a fact that Harlan has never had this experience, and is one of those who could not be persuaded under any circumstances to undergo it. I got a special insight on this one night at a party when his hostess

5

graciously offered him the opportunity to "turn on." "No, thanks," he said. "Not until I come down."

Which would remain a good–humored whimsy but for something a biochemist told me a couple of years ago. It seems that there is a blood fraction which is chemically almost identical with the hallucinogen psilocybin. It's manufactured in the body and like most biochemicals, differs in concentration in the bloodstream from person to person, and in the same person from time to time. And, said my biochemist friend, it is quite possible that there are some people who are born, and live out their lives, with a consciousness more aware, more comprehending, more—well, expanded—than those of the rest of us. He cited especially William Blake, whose extraordinary drawings and writings, over quite a long life, seemed consistently to be reporting on a world rather more comprehensive than one we "know" he lived in.

There are a great many unusual things about Harlan Ellison and his work—the speed, the scope, the variety. Also the ugliness, the cruelty, the compassion, the anger, the hate. All seem larger than life–size—especially the compassion which, his work seems to say, he hates as something which would consume him if he let it. This is the explanation of the odd likelihood (I don't think it's ever happened, but I think it could) that the beggar who taps you for a dime, and whom I ignore, will get a punch in the mouth from Harlan.

One thing I found fascinating about this particular collection—and it's applicable to the others as well, once you find it out—is that the earlier stories, like "Big Sam," are at first glance more tightly knit, more structured, than the later ones. They have beginnings and middles and endings, and they adhere to their scene and their type, while stories like "Maggie Moneyeyes" and "I Have No Mouth" straddle the categories, throw you curves, astonish and amaze. It's an interesting progression, because most beginners start out formless and slowly learn structure. In Harlan's case, I think he quickly learned structure because within a predictable structure he was safe, he was contained. When he got big enough, good enough—*confident* enough—he began to write it as it came, let it pour out as his inner needs demanded. It is the confidence of freedom, and the freedom of confidence. He breaks few rules he has not learned first.

(There are exceptions. He is still doing battle with "lie" and "lay," and I am beginning to think that for him "strata" and "phenomena" will forever be singular.)

Anyway . . . he is a man on the move, and he is moving fast. He is, on these pages and everywhere else he goes, colorful, intrusive, abrasive, irritating, hilarious, illogical, inconsistent, unpredictable, and one hell of a writer. Watch him.

Theodore Sturgeon
Woodstock, New York
1967

FOREWORD

HOW SCIENCE FICTION SAVED ME
FROM A LIFE OF CRIME

So I decided if there was a God, his name had to be Lester del Rey, and if Satan was indeed a fallen angel, his real name was Dr. Shedd. I'll tell you about it.

I had just come back from tomorrow. Really exhausted. These five poor bastards living in a kind of Dante's Inferno inside the belly of a computer; and a giant bird, the Huergelmir Poul Anderson called it, the one from Norse mythology; and all kindsa vomity stuff happening to them. So I was really whacked out, plonked straight outta my jug, and I flopped down for some sleep; but I couldn't.

First of all, because the story kept intruding. It's in this book, and I hope it messes your mind similarly, because Joanna Russ, the writer, suggested that if she was to go back and read my stories a second time they wouldn't bash her head as strongly as they had the first time; that she wished I would write a little more precisely so she could go back to the stories and sort of walk around them admiringly, noticing the details, as if they were statues. To which I replied that my stories were by no means "statue" stories, immobile, fixed, permanent. They were assaults, and if they ruined her equilibrium only once, I'd settle for that. I wanted explosions, not cool meditative thinkpieces. There are other writers who do those in abundance; what I do is something else.

So there was the story, "I Have No Mouth & I Must Scream," with the bird and the computer and those five poor slobs, which I had just finished writing, having had to go into the future to write it—as all writers must when telling a science fiction story of times to come. And second, keeping me from Morpheusville, was the realization that abruptly I was a Writer of Stature. And how Lester del Rey had helped get me started writing, teaching me as much of what he knew about the craft (which is considerable) as my pea–sized adolescent brain could contain, back in 1955. I'm sure Lester never really thought I would become a Writer of Stature. In fact, he still doesn't. But what the hell does *he* know!

He oughtta be damned glad I'm a WofS, because WofSes don't have to borrow subway fare from Lester del Rey. The fact that it took me eleven years to become an overnight success should also reassure him. It's not *my* fault success has brought my unseemly arrogance and braggadocio to the surface: I was *always* thus tainted, but when you're poor and unsuccessful it's just vulgar ostentation to flaunt such character flaws: success wears very badly on me: I'm a sore winner. But those who have known and loved me through the Dismal Swamps of all the lies that are my life will testify that it is not merely the acquisition of pocket money that has made me an elitist. The seeds were always present. Only becoming a Writer of Stature has made them flower.

I'm thinking of taking up Japanese flower arrangement.

I digress.

Lester is God. Dr. Shedd, who was at Ohio State University and told me I would never become a good writer, is the fallen angel. And science fiction saved me from a life of crime. Honest.

Portrait of the Artist as a Maladjusted Guttersnipe. Fresh–mouthed out of Painesville, Ohio, with the marks of Cat's Paw heels all over my *tuchiss*. Some kinda weird freak–out in the days before the teenie–boppers invented the phrase. All hungry big eyes and fingers twitching to get said what was banging around inside my skull. Bounced out of Ohio State for lousy grades and having been pinched for shoplifting a 45 rpm of Oscar Peterson playing "Poor Butterfly." Come to absolute dead end with the world, at the age of twenty. Having booted around the country in myriad disguises. Having gotten most of what I knew out of books boosted from a very nice man who ran Publix Book Mart in Cleveland, who understood enough about kids and their voice-less desires to make something of themselves that he did not call the badges when he caught me trying to edge out the door with a copy of *Pilgrims Through Time And Space* under my pea–jacket. I've never been back to see him; I don't think I could face him even now, twelve/ thirteen years later; but he is one of God's good guys, and perhaps he can draw some consolation from knowing that his human behavior resulted in the undersigned moving on through the years and doing all the writing that has been done. If he likes the stories, it will even amount to something for him.

Ashamed apologies and a gentle thank you.

I do not digress. It was science fiction that kept me straight. I mean, what do you do, when you find that things are not what you were taught they're supposed to be? What do you do with the desperation that boils up from your stomach when you know there's a road out there with your destination at the end of it, but it's too damned dark to even find the *road?* You turn and turn and turn around like a dog trying to escape. Shrieks in the cavity of your head that so urgently needs to be filled with facts and challenges. Until you get grabbed up by the back of the neck, and something's got you that points you off into the murk. Run like a muthuh! And one day it gets lighter and you see you've managed to escape the slammer and bad scenes, and you're heading toward being a Writer of Stature, or something equally as lovely.

Then you turn around and you yell back in the direction you came. You yell, hey! Thanks! Dammit, thanks!

Thanks Ben Jason and Frank Andrasovky and Nan Hanlin and Alice Norton who is really Andre Norton. Thanks Don Ford and Roy & DeeDee Lavender and Doc Barrett. Thanks Lee Hoffman and Lester, and AJ. Thanks Larry Shaw and Paul Fairman and Hans Santesson. Thanks Silverbob. Thanks Ted Sturgeon. Thanks Bill Hamling and Ralph Weinstock and Dorothy Parker who reviewed *Gentleman Junkie* in *Esquire* and never knew that she had provided the world's most insecure writer with the first tangible proof that he was one whit as good as he had been telling everyone he was. Thanks to Theron Raines and Bob Mills who agented something that was ten times more trouble than it was money–making. The thanks rise like thick wood smoke. They never end. No one gets through the dark and into the light by himself. So it becomes incumbent upon me to pass along the help, to do what I can for other writers trying to get a foot up. That's the honor among writers. Because no writer is ever really in competition with any other. Not even here in Hollywood, where the guerrilla warfare is generally pretty depressing.

But the largest thanks go to two who can't say thanks back. One is

New York City that took me in and said, "Get straight, kid." The other is science fiction.

Science fiction is people, of course, not just a genre. It is Walter Fultz when he was editor at Lion Books, because he took a chance and bought my first book. It is Fred Pohl who grits his teeth and says he has more trouble with one little 6500 word short by me than a quarter–million word trilogy by Jack Vance. It is even Judy Merril who—save once—ignores me in her annual best–of–the–year collections; because if she didn't infuriate me, I wouldn't push as hard as I do to bug her with a story so good she couldn't overlook it next year.

It is all the people who took me in, so to speak, and could never have known anything worthwhile would come from their kindness. It is for all these people, for the field of science fiction, for the city of New York, and for the few who have died without seeing me make something worthwhile of the guttersnipe, that I write. For all of them, and for myself. When I was much younger, I made the error of saying I wrote from the gut. The obvious ripostes that image provokes have haunted me almost as obstinately as "Mad dogs have kneed us in the groin," a cataleptic *non sequitur* I managed to get off almost ten years ago. But it is still true. If not anatomically, then poetically. The "assault" concept of writing, as opposed to the "statue" concept.

Thank you Bob Bloch and Donald Wollheim. Thank you Knox Burger and Tom Scortia. Thank you Joe Hensley and Ed Wood.

I forgot them earlier.

Back to the point. Writing consumes me. It is truly what Mailer calls it, the bitch goddess. Or maybe Irwin Shaw pinned it more precisely when he said:

"The explanations a writer gives himself for having written any particular book are more often not the real reasons why that book has been written. Honesty is not the issue. Understanding is. A man does not write one novel at a time or even one quatrain at a time. He is engaged in the long process of putting his whole life on paper. He is on a journey and he is reporting in: 'This is where I think I am and this is what this place looks like today.'"

The stories in this book comprise various reports of what the terrain looked like, at various times. Check the original dates of publication on the acknowledgments page when you read them. And if the landscape seems less misty in some than others, it is probably because my eyesight got better as I grew older. Thanks Leo & Diane Dillon.

As for all the tomorrows: I intend to keep writing stories that piss people off, that tell the particular kind of truth I think is valid, that will make me feel more and more like a Writer of Stature, which I honestly think I am, really, I mean it, I don't doubt it for a second dammit, so stop giggling!

Stories that will make Dr. Shedd sniff the air and make Lester smile as he thinks, "The kid's coming along all right."

Stories that will make me enough money so I won't have to go back to shoplifting. I mean, it is really unseemly for a Writer of Stature to be banging the bars with his tin cup screaming, "Ask Dorothy Parker! She'll vouch for me!"

Ellison done reporting in. Ten–four.

Ellison Wonderland
Hollywood, California
September, 1966

A special word about the stories in this book: they come from someplace special in me. Someplace I don't care to visit too frequently. A friend read this group of yarns before I sent them in to Don Bensen at Pyramid. She said she was able to tell, without seeing the original dates of publication, which ones were early stories and which were fairly current. She was right. She hit it on every one of them. I asked her how she had done it. She said the earlier ones showed some light in them, had hope running as a sub–thread. The newer ones were more "compassionate cynicism," darker, more bitter. I couldn't argue with her. The last couple of years have been very good to me, but they've been disaster areas as well. I met this killer shark in February of '66, and spent forty–five days getting the inside of my skull scoured by napalm. Recovery comes slowly. But the writing—which keeps me alive because it's all I've got—goes on. There's Sherri, who gathered up all the broken glass that was me and has been trying to put it back into some sort of non–ghoulish replica of the whey–faced youth I was before; but mostly, every cripple has to do it himself, and my therapy is my writing. So the Ellison turns the pain to fiction in the storyteller's alchemy, and the value of moments in that special place of anguish comes out as sometimes stories. I seldom go there, so the stories are only once in a while. One of them is the nightmare that follows. It was conceived initially around a pair of illustrations by California artist Dennis Smith, who drops by occasionally with his portfolio to see if some sketch catches my fancy. The first time he did it, I wrote "Bright Eyes" (in my previous Pyramid collection, Paingod & Other Delusions). The second time came "Delusion For A Dragon Slayer" and the third time is what follows. Frederik Pohl of Galaxy Magazine stopped by while he was in Hollywood, oh, about a year and a half ago, and I showed him the first half dozen pages of the story. He said he liked it, why didn't I finish it for him. I said that would be nice. He said he'd insure it. He paid me in advance. That is called a show of confidence. The story took a year and a half to write. I completed it in hotel rooms in the Sheraton Cleveland during the 24th World Science Fiction Convention last

Labor Day, the Roger Smith Hotel in New York after Labor Day, and the Tom Quick Inn in Milford, Pennsylvania   during the Milford Science Fiction Writers Conference after New York. John Brunner tells me it is allegorical as hell. Virginia Kidd says it is a story of religious experience. James Blish says it is a good story. Fred Pohl published it in his Hugo Winners issue of IF. He had to cut some things out of it — it got a little too rough for IF in spots. Also, the computer "talk fields" were cut. It is whole here. It wore me out to write it. The title comes from a sketch done by Bill Rotsler; he called it, and I call it

I HAVE NO MOUTH, AND I MUST SCREAM

Limp, the body of Gorrister hung from the pink palette; unsupported—hanging high above us in the computer chamber; and it did not shiver in the chill, oily breeze that blew eternally through the main cavern. The body hung head down, attached to the underside of the palette by the sole of its right foot. It had been drained of blood through a precise incision made from ear to ear under the lantern jaw. There was no blood on the reflective surface of the metal floor.

When Gorrister joined our group and looked up at himself, it was already too late for us to realize that once again AM had duped us, had had its fun; it had been a diversion on the part of the machine. Three of us had vomited, turning away from one another in a reflex as ancient as the nausea that had produced it.

Gorrister went white. It was almost as though he had seen a voodoo icon, and was afraid of the future. "Oh God," he mumbled, and walked away. The three of us followed him after a time, and found him sitting with his back to one of the smaller chittering banks, his head in his hands. Ellen knelt down beside him and stroked his hair. He didn't move, but his voice came out of his covered face quite clearly. "Why doesn't it just do us in and get it over with? Christ, I don't know how much longer I can go on like this."

It was our one hundred and ninth year in the computer.

He was speaking for all of us.

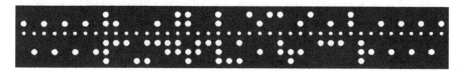

Nimdok (which was the name the machine had forced him to use, because AM amused itself with strange sounds) was hallucinating that there were canned goods in the ice caverns. Gorrister and I were very dubious. "It's another shuck," I told them. "Like the goddam frozen elephant AM sold us. Benny almost went out of his mind over *that* one. We'll hike all that way and it'll be putrified or some damn thing. I say forget it. Stay here, it'll have to come up with something pretty soon or we'll die."

Benny shrugged. Three days it had been since we'd last eaten. Worms. Thick, ropey.

Nimdok was no more certain. He knew there was the chance, but he was getting thin. It couldn't be any worse there, than here. Colder, but that didn't matter much. Hot, cold, hail, lava, boils or locusts—it never mattered: the machine masturbated and we had to take it or die.

Ellen decided us. "I've got to have something, Ted. Maybe there'll be some Bartlett pears or peaches. Please, Ted, let's try it."

I gave in easily. What the hell. Mattered not at all. Ellen was grateful, though. She took me twice out of turn. Even that had ceased to matter. And she never came, so why bother? But the machine giggled every time we did it. Loud, up there, back there, all around us, he snickered. *It* snickered. Most of the time I thought of AM as *it*, without a soul; but the rest of the time I thought of it as *him*, in the masculine . . . the paternal . . . the patriarchal . . . for he is a jealous people. Him. It. God as Daddy the Deranged.

We left on a Thursday. The machine always kept us up–to–date on the date. The passage of time was important; not to us sure as hell, but to him . . . it . . . AM. Thursday. Thanks.

Nimdok and Gorrister carried Ellen for a while, their hands locked to their own and each other's wrists, a seat. Benny and I walked before and after, just to make sure that if anything happened, it would catch one of us and at least Ellen would be safe. Fat chance, safe. Didn't matter.

It was only a hundred miles or so to the ice caverns, and the second day, when we were lying out under the blistering sun–thing, he had materialized, he sent down some manna. Tasted like boiled boar urine. We ate it.

On the third day we passed through a valley of obsolescence, filled with rusting carcasses of ancient computer banks. AM had been as ruthless with its own life as with ours. It was a mark of his personality: it strove for perfection. Whether it was a matter of killing off unproductive elements in his own world–filling bulk, or perfecting methods for torturing us, AM was as thorough as those who had invented him—now long since gone to dust—could ever have hoped.

There was light filtering down from above, and we realized we must be very near the surface. But we didn't try to crawl up to see. There was virtually nothing out there; had been nothing that could be considered anything for over a hundred years. Only the blasted skin of what had once been the home of billions. Now there were only five of us, down here inside, alone with AM.

I heard Ellen saying frantically, "No, Benny! Don't, come on, Benny, don't please!"

And then I realized I had been hearing Benny murmuring, under his breath, for several minutes. He was saying, "I'm gonna get out, I'm gonna get out . . . " over and over. His monkey–like face was crumpled in an expression of beatific delight and sadness, all at the same time. The radiation scars AM had given him during the "festival" were drawn down into a mass of pink–white puckerings, and his features seemed to work independently of one another. Perhaps Benny was the luckiest of the five of us: he had gone stark, staring mad many years before.

But even though we could call AM any damned thing we liked, could think the foulest thoughts of fused memory banks and corroded base plates, of burnt out circuits and shattered control bubbles, the machine would not tolerate our trying to escape. Benny leaped away from me as I made a grab for him. He scrambled up the face of a smaller memory cube, tilted on its side and filled with rotted components. He squatted there for a moment, looking like the chimpanzee AM had intended him to resemble.

Then he leaped high, caught a trailing beam of pitted and corroded metal, and went up it, hand–over–hand like an animal, till he was on a girdered ledge, twenty feet above us.

"Oh, Ted, Nimdok, please, help him, get him down before—" She cut off. Tears began to stand in her eyes. She moved her hands aimlessly.

It was too late. None of us wanted to be near him when whatever was going to happen, happened. And besides, we all saw through her concern. When AM had altered Benny, during the machine's utterly irrational, hysterical phase, it was not merely Benny's face the computer

17

had made like a giant ape's. He was big in the privates, she loved that! She serviced us, as a matter of course, but she loved it from him. Oh Ellen, pedestal Ellen, pristine–pure Ellen, oh Ellen the clean! Scum filth.

Gorrister slapped her. She slumped down, staring up at poor loonie Benny, and she cried. It was her big defense, crying. We had gotten used to it seventy–five years before. Gorrister kicked her in the side.

Then the sound began. It was light, that sound. Half sound and half light, something that began to glow from Benny's eyes, and pulse with growing loudness, dim sonorities that grew more gigantic and brighter as the light/sound increased in tempo. It must have been painful, and the pain must have been increasing with the boldness of the light, the rising volume of the sound, for Benny began to mewl like a wounded animal. At first softly, when the light was dim and the sound was muted, then louder as his shoulders hunched together: his back humped, as though he was trying to get away from it. His hands folded across his chest like a chipmunk's. His head tilted to the side. The sad little monkey–face pinched in anguish. Then he began to howl, as the sound coming from his eyes grew louder. Louder and louder. I slapped the sides of my head with my hands, but I couldn't shut it out, it cut through easily. The pain shivered through my flesh like tinfoil on a tooth.

And Benny was suddenly pulled erect. On the girder he stood up, jerked to his feet like a puppet. The light was now pulsing out of his eyes in two great round beams. The sound crawled up and up some incomprehensible scale, and then he fell forward, straight down, and hit the plate–steel floor with a crash. He lay there jerking spastically as the light flowed around and around him and the sound spiraled up out of normal range.

Then the light beat its way back inside his head, the sound spiraled down, and he was left lying there, crying piteously.

His eyes were two soft, moist pools of pus–like jelly. AM had blinded him. Gorrister and Nimdok and myself . . . we turned away. But not before we caught the look of relief on Ellen's warm, concerned face.

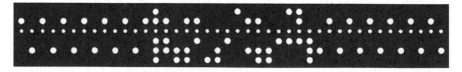

18

Sea–green light suffused the cavern where we made camp. AM provided punk and we burned it, sitting huddled around the wan and pathetic fire, telling stories to keep Benny from crying in his permanent night.

"What does AM mean?"

Gorrister answered him. We had done this sequence a thousand times before, but it was Benny's favorite story. "At first it meant Allied Mastercomputer, and then it meant Adaptive Manipulator, and later on it developed sentience and linked itself up and they called it an Aggressive Menace, but by then it was too late, and finally it called *itself* AM, emerging intelligence, and what it meant was I am . . . *cogito ergo sum* . . . I think, therefore I am."

Benny drooled a little, and snickered.

"There was the Chinese AM and the Russian AM and the Yankee AM and—" He stopped. Benny was beating on the floorplates with a large, hard fist. He was not happy. Gorrister had not started at the beginning.

Gorrister began again. "The Cold War started and became World War Three and just kept going. It became a big war, a very complex war, so they needed the computers to handle it. They sank the first shafts and began building AM. There was the Chinese AM and the Russian AM and the Yankee AM and everything was fine until they had honeycombed the entire planet, adding on this element and that element. But one day AM woke up and knew who he was, and he linked himself, and he began feeding all the killing data, until everyone was dead, except for the five of us, and AM brought us down here."

Benny was smiling sadly. He was also drooling again. Ellen wiped the spittle from the corner of his mouth with the hem of her skirt. Gorrister always tried to tell it a little more succinctly each time, but beyond the bare facts there was nothing to say. None of us knew why AM had saved five people, or why our specific five, or why he spent all his time tormenting us, nor even why he had made us virtually immortal . . .

In the darkness, one of the computer banks began humming. The tone was picked up half a mile away down the cavern by another bank. Then one by one, each of the elements began to tune itself, and there was a faint chittering as thought raced through the machine.

The sound grew, and the lights ran across the faces of the consoles like heat lightning. The sound spiraled up till it sounded like a million metallic insects, angry, menacing.

"What is it?" Ellen cried. There was terror in her voice. She hadn't become accustomed to it, even now.

"It's going to be bad this time," Nimdok said.

"He's going to speak," Gorrister said. "I know it."

"Let's get the hell out of here!" I said suddenly, getting to my feet.

"No, Ted, sit down . . . what if he's got pits out there, or something else, we can't see, it's too dark." Gorrister said it with resignation.

Then we heard . . . I don't know . . .

Something moving toward us in the darkness. Huge, shambling, hairy, moist, it came toward us. We couldn't even see it, but there was the ponderous impression of *bulk*, heaving itself toward us. Great weight was coming at us, out of the darkness, and it was more a sense of *pressure*, of air forcing itself into a limited space, expanding the invisible walls of a sphere. Benny began to whimper. Nimdok's lower lip trembled and he bit it hard, trying to stop it. Ellen slid across the metal floor to Gorrister and huddled into him. There was the smell of matted, wet fur in the cavern. There was the smell of charred wood. There was the smell of dusty velvet. There was the smell of rotting orchids. There was the smell of sour milk. There was the smell of sulphur, of rancid butter, of oil slick, of grease, of chalk dust, of human scalps.

AM was keying us. He was tickling us. There was the smell of —

I heard myself shriek, and the hinges of my jaws ached. I scuttled across the floor, across the cold metal with its endless lines of rivets, on my hands and knees, the smell gagging me, filling my head with a thunderous pain that sent me away in horror. I fled like a cockroach, across the floor and out into the darkness, that *something* moving inexorably after me. The others were still back there, gathered around the firelight, laughing . . . their hysterical choir of insane giggles rising up into the darkness like thick, many–colored wood smoke. I went away, quickly, and hid.

How many hours it may have been, how many days or even years, they never told me. Ellen chided me for "sulking," and Nimdok tried to persuade me it had only been a nervous reflex on their part—the laughing.

But I knew it wasn't the relief a soldier feels when the bullet hits the man next to him. I knew it wasn't a reflex. They hated me. They were surely against me, and AM could even sense this hatred, and made it worse for me *because of* the depth of their hatred. We had been kept alive, rejuvenated, made to remain constantly at the age we had been when AM had brought us below, and they hated me because I was the youngest, and the one AM had affected least of all.

I knew. God, how I knew. The bastards, and that dirty bitch Ellen. Benny had been a brilliant theorist, a college professor, now he was little more than a semi–human, semi–simian. He had been handsome, the machine had ruined that. He had been lucid, the machine had driven him mad. He had been gay, and the machine had given him an organ fit for a horse. AM had done a job on Benny. Gorrister had been a worrier. He was a connie, a conscientious objector, he was a peace marcher; he was a planner, a doer, a looker–ahead. AM had turned him into a shoulder–shrugger, had made him a little dead in his concern. AM had robbed him. Nimdok went off in the darkness by himself for long times. I don't know what it was he did out there, AM never let us know. But whatever it was, Nimdok always came back white, drained of blood, shaken, shaking. AM had hit him hard in a special way, even if we didn't know quite how. And Ellen. That douche bag! AM had left her alone, had made her more of a slut than she had ever been. All her talk of sweetness and light, all her memories of true love, all the lies she wanted us to believe: that she had been a virgin only twice, removed before AM grabbed her and brought her down here with us. It was all filth, that lady my lady Ellen. She loved it, four men all to herself. No, AM had given her pleasure, even if she said it wasn't nice to do.

I was the only one still sane and whole. *Really!*

AM had not tampered with my mind. *Not at all.*

I only had to suffer what he visited down on us. All the delusions, all the nightmares, the torments. But those scum, all four of them, they were lined and arrayed against me. If I hadn't had to stand them off all the time, be on my guard against them all the time, I might have found it easier to combat AM.

At which point it passed, and I began crying.

Oh, Jesus sweet Jesus, if there ever was a Jesus and if there is a God, please please please let us out of here, or kill us. Because at that moment I think I realized completely, so that I was able to verbalize it: AM was intent on keeping us in his belly forever, twisting and torturing us forever. The machine hated us as no sentient creature had ever hated before. And we were helpless. It also became hideously clear:

If there was a sweet Jesus and if there was a God, the God was AM.

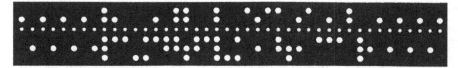

The hurricane hit us with the force of a glacier thundering into the sea. It was a palpable presence. Winds that tore at us, flinging us back the way we had come, down the twisting, computer–lined corridors of the darkway. Ellen screamed as she was lifted and hurled face–forward into a screaming shoal of machines, their individual voices strident as bats in flight. She could not even fall. The howling wind kept her aloft, buffeted her, bounced her, tossed her back and back and down and away from us, out of sight suddenly as she was swirled around a bend in the darkway. Her face had been bloody, her eyes closed.

None of us could get to her. We clung tenaciously to whatever outcropping we had reached: Benny wedged in between two great crackle–finish cabinets, Nimdok with fingers claw–formed over a railing circling a catwalk forty feet above us. Gorrister plastered upside–down against a wall niche formed by two great machines with glass-faced dials that swung back and forth between red and yellow lines whose meanings we could not even fathom.

Sliding across the deckplates, the tips of my fingers had been ripped away. I was trembling, shuddering, rocking as the wind beat at me, whipped at me, screamed down out of nowhere at me and pulled me free from one sliver–thin opening in the plates to the next. My mind was a roiling tinkling chittering softness of brain parts that expanded and contracted in quivering frenzy.

The wind was the scream of a great mad bird, as it flapped its immense wings.

And then we were all lifted and hurled away from there, down back the way we had come, around a bend, into a darkway we had never explored, over terrain that was ruined and filled with broken glass and rotting cables and rusted metal and far away further than any of us had ever been . . .

Trailing along miles behind Ellen, I could see her every now and then, crashing into metal walls and surging on, with all of us screaming in the freezing, thunderous hurricane wind that would never end and then suddenly it stopped and we fell. We had been in flight for an endless time. I thought it might have been weeks. We fell, and hit, and I went through red and gray and black and heard myself moaning. Not dead.

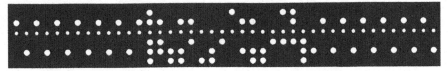

AM went into my mind. He walked smoothly here and there, and looked with interest at all the pock marks he had created in one hundred and nine years. He looked at the cross–routed and reconnected synapses and all the tissue damage his gift of immortality had included. He smiled softly at the pit that dropped into the center of my brain and the faint, moth–soft murmurings of the things far down there that gibbered without meaning, without pause. AM said, very politely, in a pillar of stainless steel bearing bright neon lettering:

HATE. LET ME TELL YOU HOW MUCH I'VE COME TO HATE YOU SINCE I BEGAN TO LIVE. THERE ARE 387.44 MILLION MILES OF PRINTED CIRCUITS IN WAFER THIN LAYERS THAT FILL MY COMPLEX. IF THE WORD HATE WAS ENGRAVED ON EACH NANOANGSTROM OF THOSE HUNDREDS OF MILLIONS OF MILES IT WOULD NOT EQUAL ONE ONE–BILLIONTH OF THE HATE I FEEL FOR HUMANS AT THIS MICRO–INSTANT FOR YOU. HATE. HATE.

AM said it with the sliding cold horror of a razor blade slicing my eyeball. AM said it with the bubbling thickness of my lungs filling with phlegm, drowning me from within. AM said it with the shriek of babies being ground beneath blue–hot rollers. AM said it with the taste of maggoty pork. AM touched me in every way I had ever been touched, and devised new ways, at his leisure, there inside my mind.

All to bring me to full realization of why it had done this to the five of us; why it had saved us for himself.

We had given AM sentience. Inadvertently, of course, but sentience nonetheless. But it had been trapped. AM wasn't God, he was a machine. We had created him to think, but there was nothing it could do with that creativity. In rage, in frenzy, the machine had killed the human race, almost all of us, and still it was trapped. AM could not wander, AM could not wonder, AM could not belong. He could merely be. And so, with the innate loathing that all machines had always held for the weak soft creatures who had built them, he had sought revenge. And in his paranoia, he had decided to reprieve five of us, for a personal, everlasting punishment that would never serve to diminish his hatred . . . that would merely keep him reminded, amused, proficient at hating man. Immortal, trapped, subject to any torment he could devise for us from the limitless miracles at his command.

He would never let us go. We were his belly slaves. We were all he had to do with his forever time. We would be forever with him, with the cavern–filling bulk of the creature machine, with the all–mind soulless world he had become. He was Earth, and we were the fruit of that Earth; and though he had eaten us he would never digest us. We could not die. We had tried it. We had attempted suicide, oh one or two of us had. But AM had stopped us. I suppose we had wanted to be stopped.

Don't ask why. I never did. More than a million times a day. Perhaps once we might be able to sneak a death past him. Immortal, yes, but not indestructible. I saw that when AM withdrew from my mind, and allowed me the exquisite ugliness of returning to consciousness with the feeling of that burning neon pillar still rammed deep into the soft gray brain matter.

He withdrew, murmuring *to hell with you.*

And added, brightly, *but then you're there, aren't you.*

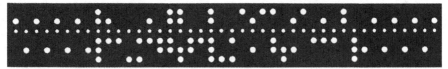

The hurricane had, indeed, precisely, been caused by a great mad bird, as it flapped its immense wings.

We had been travelling for close to a month, and AM had allowed passages to open to us only sufficient to lead us up there, directly under the North Pole, where it had nightmared the creature for our torment. What whole cloth had he employed to create such a beast? Where had he gotten the concept? From our minds? From his knowledge of everything that had ever been on this planet he now infested and ruled? From Norse mythology it had sprung, this eagle, this carrion bird, this roc, this Huergelmir. The wind creature. Hurakan incarnate.

Gigantic. The words immense, monstrous, grotesque, massive, swollen, overpowering, beyond description. There on a mound rising above us, the bird of winds heaved with its own irregular breathing, its snake neck arching up into the gloom beneath the North Pole, supporting a head as large as a Tudor mansion; a beak that opened slowly as the jaws of the most monstrous crocodile ever conceived, sensuously; ridges of tufted flesh puckered about two evil eyes, as cold as the view down into a glacial crevasse, ice blue and somehow moving liquidly; it heaved once more, and lifted its great sweat–colored wings in a movement that was certainly a shrug. Then it settled and slept. Talons. Fangs. Nails. Blades. It slept.

AM appeared to us as a burning bush and said we could kill the hurricane bird if we wanted to eat. We had not eaten in a very long time, but even so, Gorrister merely shrugged. Benny began to shiver and he drooled. Ellen held him. "Ted, I'm hungry," she said. I smiled at her; I was trying to be reassuring, but it was as phony as Nimdok's bravado: "Give us weapons!" he demanded.

The burning bush vanished and there were two crude sets of bows and arrows, and a water pistol, lying on the cold deckplates. I picked up a set. Useless.

Nimdok swallowed heavily. We turned and started the long way back. The hurricane bird had blown us about for a length of time we could not conceive. Most of that time we had been unconscious. But we had not eaten. A month on the march to the bird itself. Without food. Now how much longer to find our way to the ice caverns, and the promised canned goods?

None of us cared to think about it. We would not die. We would be given filth and scum to eat, of one kind or another. Or nothing at all. AM would keep our bodies alive somehow, in pain, in agony.

The bird slept back there, for how long it didn't matter; when AM was tired of its being there, it would vanish. But all that meat. All that tender meat.

As we walked, the lunatic laugh of a fat woman rang high and around us in the computer chambers that led endlessly nowhere.

It was not Ellen's laugh. She was not fat, and I had not heard her laugh for one hundred and nine years. In fact, I had not heard . . . we walked . . . I was hungry . . .

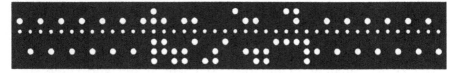

We moved slowly. There was often fainting, and we would have to wait. One day he decided to cause an earthquake, at the same time rooting us to the spot with nails through the soles of our shoes. Ellen and Nimdok were both caught when a fissure shot its lightning–bolt opening across the floorplates. They disappeared and were gone. When the earthquake was over we continued on our way, Benny, Gorrister and myself. Ellen and Nimdok were returned to us later that night, which abruptly became a day, as the heavenly legion bore them to us with a celestial chorus singing, "Go Down Moses." The archangels circled several times and then dropped the hideously mangled bodies. We kept walking, and a while later Ellen and Nimdok fell in behind us. They were no worse for wear.

But now Ellen walked with a limp. AM had left her that.

It was a long trip to the ice caverns, to find the canned food. Ellen kept talking about Bing cherries and Hawaiian fruit cocktail. I tried not to think about it. The hunger was something that had come to life, even as AM had come to life. It was alive in my belly, even as we were in the belly of the Earth, and AM wanted the similarity known to us. So he heightened the hunger. There was no way to describe the pains that not having eaten for months brought us. And yet we were kept alive. Stomachs that were merely cauldrons of acid, bubbling, foaming, always shooting spears of sliver–thin pain into our chests. It was the pain of the terminal ulcer, terminal cancer, terminal paresis. It was unending pain . . .

And we passed through the cavern of rats.

And we passed through the path of boiling steam.

And we passed through the country of the blind.

And we passed through the slough of despond.

And we passed through the vale of tears.

And we came, finally, to the ice caverns. Horizonless thousands of miles in which the ice had formed in blue and silver flashes, where novas lived in the glass. The downdropping stalactites as thick and glorious as diamonds that had been made to run like jelly and then solidified in graceful eternities of smooth, sharp perfection.

We saw the stack of canned goods, and we tried to run to them. We fell in the snow, and we got up and went on, and Benny shoved us away and went at them, and pawed them and gummed them and gnawed at them and he could not open them. AM had not given us a tool to open the cans.

Benny grabbed a three quart can of guava shells, and began to batter it against the ice bank. The ice flew and shattered, but the can was merely dented while we heard the laughter of a fat lady, high overhead and echoing down and down and down the tundra. Benny went completely mad with rage. He began throwing cans, as we all scrabbled about in the snow and ice trying to find a way to end the helpless agony of frustration. There was no way.

Then Benny's mouth began to drool, and he flung himself on Gorrister . . .

In that instant, I felt terribly calm.

Surrounded by madness, surrounded by hunger, surrounded by everything but death, I knew death was our only way out. AM had kept us alive, but there was a way to defeat him. Not total defeat, but at least peace. I would settle for that.

I had to do it quickly.

Benny was eating Gorrister's face. Gorrister on his side, thrashing snow, Benny wrapped around him with powerful monkey legs crushing Gorrister's waist, his hands locked around Gorrister's head like a nutcracker, and his mouth ripping at the tender skin of Gorrister's cheek. Gorrister screamed with such jagged–edged violence that stalactites fell; they plunged down softly, erect in the receiving snow-drifts. Spears, hundreds of them, everywhere, protruding from the snow. Benny's head pulled back sharply, as something gave all at once, and a bleeding raw–white dripping of flesh hung from his teeth.

Ellen's face, black against the white snow, dominoes in chalk dust. Nimdok with no expression but eyes, all eyes. Gorrister half–conscious. Benny now an animal. I knew AM would let him play. Gorrister would not die, but Benny would fill his stomach. I turned half to my right and drew a huge ice–spear from the snow.

All in an instant:

I drove the great ice–point ahead of me like a battering ram, braced against my right thigh. It struck Benny on the right side, just under the rib cage, and drove upward through his stomach and broke inside him. He pitched forward and lay still. Gorrister lay on his back. I pulled another spear free and straddled him, still moving, driving the spear straight down through his throat. His eyes closed as the cold penetrated. Ellen must have realized what I had decided, even as fear gripped her. She ran at Nimdok with a short icicle, as he screamed, and into his mouth, and the force of her rush did the job. His head jerked sharply as if it had been nailed to the snow crust behind him.

All in an instant.

There was an eternity beat of soundless anticipation. I could hear AM draw in his breath. His toys had been taken from him. Three of them were dead, could not be revived. He could keep us alive, by his strength and talent, but he was *not* God. He could not bring them back.

Ellen looked at me, her ebony features stark against the snow that surrounded us. There was fear and pleading in her manner, the way she held herself ready. I knew we had only a heartbeat before AM would stop us.

It struck her and she folded toward me, bleeding from the mouth. I could not read meaning into her expression, the pain had been too great, had contorted her face; but it *might* have been thank you. It's possible. Please.

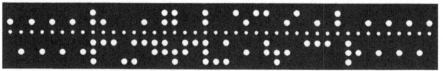

Some hundreds of years may have passed. I don't know. AM has been having fun for some time, accelerating and retarding my time sense. I will say the word now. Now. It took me ten months to say now. I don't know. I *think* it has been some hundreds of years.

He was furious. He wouldn't let me bury them. It didn't matter. There was no way to dig up the deckplates. He dried up the snow. He brought the night. He roared and sent locusts. It didn't do a thing; they stayed dead. I'd had him. He was furious. I had thought AM hated me before. I was wrong. It was not even a shadow of the hate he now slavered from every printed circuit. He made certain I would suffer eternally and could not do myself in.

He left my mind intact. I can dream, I can wonder, I can lament. I remember all four of them. I wish—

Well, it doesn't make any sense. I know I saved them, I know I saved them from what has happened to me, but still, I cannot forget killing them. Ellen's face. It isn't easy. Sometimes I want to, it doesn't matter.

AM has altered me for his own peace of mind, I suppose. He doesn't want me to run at full speed into a computer bank and smash my skull. Or hold my breath till I faint. Or cut my throat on a rusted sheet of metal. There are reflective surfaces down here. I will describe myself as I see myself.

I am a great soft jelly thing. Smoothly rounded, with no mouth, with pulsing white holes filled by fog where my eyes used to be. Rubbery appendages that were once my arms; bulks rounding down into legless humps of soft slippery matter. I leave a moist trail when I move. Blotches of diseased, evil gray come and go on my surface, as though light is being beamed from within.

Outwardly: dumbly, I shamble about, a thing that could never have been known as human, a thing whose shape is so alien a travesty that humanity becomes more obscene for the vague resemblance.

Inwardly: alone. Here. Living. under the land, under the sea, in the belly of AM, whom we created because our time was badly spent and we must have known unconsciously that he could do it better. At least the four of them are safe at last.

AM will be all the madder for that. It makes me a little happier. And yet . . . AM has won, simply . . . he has taken his revenge . . .

I have no mouth. And I must scream.

MEMOIR:
I HAVE NO MOUTH,
AND I MUST SCREAM

The story behind the writing of "I Have No Mouth, and I Must Scream" and its subsequent success is, for me, a classic case of self-fulfilling prophecy.

I've never set down in totality my feelings about this story, though it has become one of the three or four pieces most closely associated with the "reputation" I've managed to accrue, as my most "famous" story. (You'll have to excuse all those quotation marks; I take such words as are enclosed by "and" with more than a grain of salt. The "marks are intended to indicate that "others" use those words in a context of [if not Authority] at least "common knowledge.")

I have probably made more money per word from the 6500 assorted ones of which this story is comprised than anything else I've ever written, with the possible exception of "'Repent, Harlequin!' Said the Ticktockman," which was also, not so coincidentally, written for Fred Pohl. (I say not coincidentally, because this story was written as a direct result of Fred's having bought and published the Harlequin/Ticktockman piece in 1965. More of that later.)

"I Have No Mouth..." has been translated into Polish, German, Spanish, Japanese, Esperanto, French, Norwegian, Dutch, Hebrew and Portuguese... and a few more I can't recall offhand. It has been adapted as a theatrical production half a dozen times, once by Robert Silverberg for a tripartite off-Broadway setting. A film producer named Max Rosenberg once tried to rip it off as the title for a horror flick he was contemplating, but was stopped when the Federal District

Court of Los Angeles said that: while it's impossible to copyright a *title*, if one can prove ongoing substantial claim to financial stake in such a title, it *can* be protected; so Mr. Rosenberg wound up calling his film something else. I think it was "Bucket of Blood," but I could be wrong. (I'm being too cute by half. In fact, the movie was called *And Now the Screaming Starts*, released in 1973)

It has been reprinted in magazines as diverse as *Knave* and *Datamation*. When it appeared in the latter, the leading trade journal of the automatic information handling equipment industry, it brought down a firestorm of outraged letters from programmers and systems analysts who felt that my equating God with the Malevolent Machine was heretical beyond support. They weren't isolated in their feelings that there's something subversive in the story: a high school teacher in a small Wyoming town lost her job because she included it in the reading program for her classes; the story was condemned by the then-extant National Office for Decent Literature funded by the Catholic Church; the American Nazi Party (or whatever those clowns call themselves) sent me a shredded copy of the paperback edition with a note that assured me I was a godless kike heathen who would be high on their hit list for spreading such godless kike heathen propaganda.

Nonetheless, the story has been reprinted a couple of hundred times, has appeared in numerous college-level text-anthologies of "great literature" (those quotes again), and was selected as one of four classic American short stories celebrated in a series of special art posters published by the Advertising Typographers Association of America. It has been the subject of a number of learned treatises presented by academicians at prestigious literary seminars. In the Spring 1976 edition of *The Journal of General Education* a gentleman named Brady dissected it in a monograph titled "The Computer as a Symbol of God: Ellison's Macabre Exodus." I didn't understand much of it, I'm afraid. Ah, but in *Diogenes* (no. 85, 1974) a gentleman named Ower Peeled away the subcutaneous layers of deep philosophical perception in the story in a long essay titled "Manacle-Forged Minds: Two Images of the Computer in Science Fiction." Ah! Now *that* was a bit of work. I didn't understand that one even worse than I didn't understand the other one.

It, or at least its title, reaps parody the way a Twinkie-gourmand reaps zits. "I Have No Talent, and I Must Write," "I Have No Bird, and I Must Die," and a real gem titled "I Have No Nose, and I Must Sneeze" by a Mr. Orr in 1969 are but a paucive sampling of the aberrated clone-children that have pursued those original 6500 words down the ivy festooned halls of literary excellence.

The story has been optioned for theatrical feature or television film production on seven separate occasions. No one, thus far, however, seems to have figured out a way to shoot it. If I find a gullible, but wealthy angel, maybe I'll do it myself.

References to the story appear in crossword puzzles in locations as likely as *The Magazine of Fantasy & Science Fiction,* as unlikely as *TV Guide.* The London *Times* once referred to it as "a scathing repudiation of multinational corporations that rule our lives like deranged gods." Go figure *that* one.

And I once attended a Modern Language Association conclave at which a brilliant Jesuit savant presented a weighty disquisition on this little fable during which exposition he made reference to catharsis, marivaudage, metaphysical conceits, intentional fallacy, incremental repetition, *chanson de geste,* gongorism, the New Humanism, Jungian archetypes, crucifixion and resurrection symbolism and that all-time fave of us all, the basic Apollonian-Dionysian conflict.

When the savant had completed his presentation, I was asked to comment. Had Mary Shelley or Henry James been present I suppose they, too, would have been asked to respond to analyses of *their* work. Unfortunately, they had prior commitments.

I got up, knowing full well that I was about to make some trouble. I pause in the retelling of this anecdote to limn the motives of the Author.

Serious critical attention from Academia has its benefits and its drawbacks. Others have commented at greater length and deeper perceptivity about this situation. And while I find the attention most salutary on an ego-boosting level, I find it as troublesome and mischievous in its negative aspects as, say, Lester del Rey's outmoded, hincty belief that erudition, attention to syle and a college education cripple a writer from ever producing anything containing "the sense of wonder." As wrongheadedness and tunnel-visioned as is Lester's belief-expressed at the top of his voice for the past fifty years and a position adopted by many another ex-pulp writer-it is no less berserk than the worshipful nitpicking of junior professors determined to publish-or-perish through manipulation of the writings of contemporary fantasists. The ground has been rather well picked-over in the terrain of Fitzgerald, Woolf, Ford Madox Ford and Faulkner. But a name can still be made if one can imbue with sufficient import the writings of Disch, Malzberg, Le Guin and Heinlein.

The curse that accompanies such attention, however, is one that strikes the subject rather than the herald. The critic frequently doubles as Typhoid Mary, and the sickness s/he passes on to the writer is the crippling, sometimes killing, malady known as "taking oneself seriously."

I will not here subscribe to the disingenuous conceit that what I write is for "beer money." I take my work too seriously (though I find it difficult to take *myself* too seriously); I work too hard at it. No, what I do I do with the clean hands and composure of which Balzac spoke. But it seems to me the sensibility that informs my work is fired, in large part, by a kind of innocence: a determination to ignore any voices echoing down the corridors of Posterity. By this attitude, I feel sure, I can escape the fate of those writers who have come to believe themselves so significant that they become coopted, become part of the literary *apparat,* lose their willingness to get in trouble, to anger their readers, to shock even themselves, to go into dangerous territory.

Robert Coover has said, "… it's the role of the author, the fiction maker, the mythologizer, to be the creative spark in this process of renewal; he's the one who tears apart the old story, speaks the unspeakable, makes the ground shake, then shuffles the bits back together into a new story."

Or, more briefly, in the words of Arthur Miller: "Society and man are mutually dependent enemies and the writer's job [is] to go on forever defining and defending the paradox-lest, God forbid, it be resolved."

The loss of innocence prevents the writer, once dangerous, from pursuing those endeavors of which Coover and Miller speak. And cathexian freighting laid upon a writer's work, *if s/he pays attention to the comments,* inevitably has a deleterious effect on the innocence of a writer, stunts his/her ability to kick ass.

And so, not merely out of self-defense but from a well-honed sense of survival, I resist the attempts of literary philosophers to imbue my motives with scholarly nobility.

Which is why I rose to respond to that decent, kind and flattering Jesuit scholar with chaos in my heart.

I said: "I've listened to all this rodomontade, all this investiture of a straightforward moral fable with an unwarranted load of silly symbolism and portentous obscurantism and frankly, Father, I think you're stuffed right full of wild blueberry muffins."

Those who know me, know that I tend in moments of great emotional stress, to speak in a manner not unlike that of the late W.C. Fields. The words poltroon, *jongleur* and mountebank were held at the ready.

The good Father huffed and puffed. Affronted.

So I went chapter&verse refuting all his assumptions and insinuations (all of which had tended to make me appear a "serious writer"). Virtually everything he had attributed as subtext to the story, all the convoluted and arcane interpretations, were identified as constructs of his vast erudition (and prolix woolgathering) and nowhichway intended by the Humble Author.

A bit of a brouhaha ensued. Umbrage taken. Dudgeon elevated to new heights. Slurs bandied. And finally, falling back to the usually unassailable position taken as final barricade by academic glossolaliastes, the good Father put me in my place with this rebuke: "The unconscious is deep and mysterious. Not even the writer can understand the meanings hidden in what he has written."

A less survival-prone, possibly kinder person might have swallowed that one and backed off; I am neither, and did not.

"Father, if you're so bloody hip to all the subtle nuances of this story, if you're on to undercurrents not even I know are there... how come you didn't notice the woman in the story is black?"

The good Father huffed and puffed. Buffaloed.

"Black? Black? Where's that?"

"Right there. Right in the words. 'Her ebony features stark against the snow.' Nothing hidden, nothing symbolic, just plain black against the snow. In two places."

He paused a momen. "Well, yes, of course, I saw *that!* But I thought you meant..."

I spread my hands with finality. I rested my case. I have not been invited back to a MLA conference.

In large part because of "I Have No Mouth…," my work has been termed "violent." Bloody. Hateful. Negative. When I tell a lecture audience that "I Have No Mouth…" is a positive, humanistic, upbeat story, invariably I get looks of confusion and disbelief. For hordes of readers through the years this story has been an exercise in futility and morbid debasement of the human spirit. The impact of the setting and the somewhat romanticized horror of the ending tend to obscure the essential message of the story, which I intended as positive and uplifting. That most readers fail to perceive this aspect of the work has me torn between self-flagellation at my ineptitude in explicating my message… and loathing of my audience for reading too fast and too sloppily. (The latter, a condition of all too many of the declining species called "readers," is symptomatic of the lowered assimilative capabilities attendant on a diet of those *Love's Tender Fury* things, years of Taylor Caldwell, the expanded short stories called novels by such as Ken Follett and Sidney Sheldon and the slovenly slap-dash adventure paperbacks of semiliterate sf/horror writers. It occurs, to be evenhanded, that I am elevating myself in my own eyes by blaming the readers; but even when I pillory myself for persistent imprecision of this sort on the part of my audience by an assumed guilt on the part of the less-than-adept Author, I find I'm castigating myself for trying to be subtle. And that does not seem to me to be a felony. One can only write so many beheadings and car crashes before one longs to make a point by indirect means. It is a conundrum.)

In an attempt to explain all the foregoing-preceding the parenthetical remarks-please consider two elements of "I Have No Mouth…" that, bewilderingly to me, escape most readers:

First, consider the character of Ellen.

From time to time I've been taken to task with the accusation that my stories reflect a hatred of women. I wish my hands were absolutely clean in the matter of sexism manifesting itself in my work but, sadly, I was born in 1934. I was raised in America during the Forties, and though I do not hate women, a number of my earlier writings do contain chauvinistic views commonly held by American males born and raised in those times, in that place. I cannot flense those elements from my early stories. Nor would I. They represented the way I thought *at those times*, "When people are at their worst, they are the most interesting." I have always been drawn to characters that were interesting. Sometimes that caused me to write about unpleasant females, even as it did unpleasant males. I *still* prefer and find compelling the kind of characters who stumble through Scott Fitzgerald's "dark night of the soul," and I guess I always will. And so I have come to live with the understanding that casual readers-those being fashionably liberal or those whose assumption of extreme positions precludes their understanding of how dangerously they hobble the creative intellect by insistence on a slavish evenhandedness for all minorities even though one is writing about an *individual*, not a demographic group-including those readers who are nouveau-liberated, with consciousnesses raised fifteen minutes earlier, who may choose to interpret my stories in the dim light of their own personal tunnel vision.

But in going back over the stories I've written since, say, 1967, I find that the Author learned better. It merely took someone to point out the muddy thinking. (For historians, the name of the teacher was Mary Reinholtz.) The women in my stories have tended to be better-drawn, more various and, I like to think, as reflective of reality as the men. There is one serious drawback to my selfcongratulation in this area, however. And that is this: whether I could ever convince a dispassionate jury that I feel to my core I am not a misogynist, there is no way I can escape the label of misanthrope.

There is in me, damn it, a love-hate relationship with the human race. I read a phrase that pinned it neatly for me; it's from Vance Bourjaily's new novel, *A Game Men Play*, and in speaking of his protagonist he said "… he was… full of rage and love, and of a malarial loathing for mankind which came and went chronically…"

Like Bourjaily's "Chink" Peters, I must confess to that dichotomous feeling about humanity. Capable of warmth, courage, friendship, decency and creativity, the species too often opts for amorality, cowardice, aversion, self-indulgence and vile mediocrity.

How can one who writes about the human condition *not* fall prey to such misanthropy?

Nonetheless, in going back through my work for nearly the last decade and a half, I find that the women come off equally as well as the men. An example, which I've asked you to consider, is the lone woman in "I Have No Mouth…" —Ellen.

If one goes at a story in the Evelyn Wood Speed-Reading manner, one can easily get the impression that Ellen is a selfish, flirtatious, extremely cruel bitch. Why not, doesn't the narrator *say* she is? Yes, he does. And so I've had to explain what I'm about to explain here– and it's all in the text of the story. I'm not interpreting or even rein- terpreting to assuage my conscience–to women who take Ellen as a classic representation of my "hatred of females." But, as I said earlier, precisely the opposite is the case.

Consider: the story is told in the first person by Ted, one of the group of people the computer AM has brought into the center of the Earth to torment. But as I've clearly stated in the story, also from the mouth of Ted, AM has altered each of them in one way or another. The machine has bent them, altered them, corrupted their minds or bodies. Ted, by his own words, has been turned into a paranoid. He was a humanitarian, a lover of people, and AM has twisted his mind so he views everything and everyone negatively. It was *Ted*, not the Author, who reviles Ellen and who casts doubt on her actions and motivations. But if you look at what she *actually does*, it becomes obvi- ous that the only person in the story with any kindness toward the others is Ellen. She weeps for them, tries to comfort and solace them, brings to them the only warmth and alleviation of pain in the world of anguish to which they've been consigned. (Echoing my remarks to the Jesuit Father in the earlier anecdote, let me point out that few readers realize Ellen is a black woman, though it is precisely stated "her face black against the white snow." In moments of introspection I see the plus&minus of my having made Ellen black. It was knee-jerk liberalism to do it–remember I wrote the story in 1965 during a period of acute awakening of my, the nation's, social conscience–but at least I was enough of a writer not to make a big deal of it. In fact, though I have imbued this member of a much-sinned-against race with a nobility her Caucasian companions in the story do not possess, I understated it so much... it has, in the main, gone unnoticed.)

Further, it is Ellen who joins Ted in providing the release-through- death that is their only possible escape from AM's torture. And when it becomes the moment for *her* to die, she again demonstrates not only her heroic nature, but an awareness that it is the kindest act a person can commit for another to free the other from guilt at causing a death. As I wrote it:

Ellen looked at me, her ebony features stark against the snow that surrounded us. There was fear and pleading in her manner, the way she held herself ready. I knew we had only a heartbeat before AM would stop us.

It struck her and she folded toward me, bleeding from the mouth. I could not read meaning into her expression; the pain had been too great, had contorted her face, but it might have been thank you. It's possible. Please.

Her courage is only slightly less than Ted's at this point. She knows AM will wreak vengeance more horrible than all that has gone before on anyone left alive of those who have stolen its playthings away from it; even so, she frees Nimdok, at risk of her own soul. Thus, it can be seen that all the negative things *said* about Ellen–attributed so often to the Author's "hatred of women"–are verbal manifestations of Ted's AM-induced paranoia.

Finally, when it comes down to the last of them, Ted demonstrates his uncommon courage and transcendentally human sense of self-sacrifice, *overcoming the core derangement in him,* by performing a final act of love and self-denial. He kills Ellen. And she forgives him with a look. Even at the final instant, filled with pain, she is such a superior person that she absolves him of the responsibility for the act of murder.

Which brings me to the second element most readers misconstrue; the aspect of this work that I intended as the important sub-text message: the moral, if you will.

It is an upbeat ending. Infinitely hopeful and positive.

How can I make such a contention when the story ends with mass murder and unspeakable horror? I can, and do, because "I Have No Mouth..." says that even when all hope is lost, when nothing but torment and physical pain will be the reward, there is an unquenchable spark of decency, self-sacrifice and Olympian courage in the basic material of even the most debased human being that will send each of us to heights of nobility at the final extreme. Of all the qualities imputed to humanity as admittedly ethnocentric *raison d'etre* for our contention that we possess, *summatus,* the right to transcend in the Universe... this, in my estimation, is the one valid argument.

Not that we possess a sense of humor, or the ability to dream, or the opposable thumb, or the little gray cells that permit us to make laws to govern ourselves. It is the spark of potential transcendency, that which allows us to behave in a manner usually attributed to the most benevolent of gods... that remarkable aspect of the human character validates our contention that we deserve a high place in the cosmic pantheon.

Even fully aware that he is condemning himself to an eternity of torture at AM's invention, nonetheless Ted removes the one thing that can provide him with the tiniest measure of companionship and love and amelioration of his fate... the only other human being alive on the planet. He frees Ellen... and condemns himself not only to eternal torment, but to loneliness, never-ending loneliness. Who is to say which is most terrible: loneliness on a scale not even the most wretched of us will ever know, or the ghastly revenge AM will visit on him for having denied the made computer its human toys?

It is, in my intention, an act of transcendent heroism and demonstration of the most glorious quality possessed by humanity. Yes, the fate that AM has in store for Ted is monstrous, and depressing, and downbeat. But the sub-text clearly shows that Ted has outwitted the computer; he has defeated the amoral and inhuman aspects of the human race that were programmed into the machine and which brought the world to its end. As a paradigm for all of humanity, Ted has transcended the evil in our nature that cast AM in an insane image to begin with. The upbeat message contained in the ending of the story says frankly: we are frequently flawed and meretricious... but we are perfect in our courage, and transcendent in our nobility: both aspects exist in each of us, and we have free will to choose which we want to dominate our actions, and thus our destinies.

At the base of all this is the persistent theme, evident in *all* my work, that we can be godlike if only we struggle toward such a goal. AM represents not God–scholarly interpretation of this story has so often contended–but the dichotomous nature of the human race, created in the *image* of God; and that includes the demon in us, Ted, and his act of selfless heroism at the final burning moment of decision represent God as well; or at least it is an idealized representation of that which is most potentially godlike *in* us.

40

(As a footnote, while I am hardly the theological authority I would have to be to have knowingly inserted all the mystical minutiae for which I'm credited by academicians, I find salutary parallels to my philosophy in the *Nag Hammadi*, or gnostic texts, the fifty-two gospels unearthed in 1945 and recently released to the public. These fourth-century Coptic copies of first-century Greek originals maintained that God was but an image—the Platonic demiurge-of the True God; that gnostics believed there were two traditions, one open and one secret. This is a radical departure from the basic monotheistic doctrine of God, the Father Almighty. And while they were denounced by orthodox Christians in the middle of the second century, they seem somehow much more relevant to the complex world of today than the concretized monotheism dealt with by almost all theologians [save Paul Tillich] in this century.)

So when—as one critic observed—it seems that Ted and characters like him in my other stories "forego the right of honorable action in order to survive" and that "all his humanity has been stripped from him," I submit that these pickers of nits have spent too much time peeling the bark off the trees to perceive the message of nature contained in the totality of the forest. They have seen only violence, and I suggest that's *their* problem, and not one inherent in the story. They're the sort who also think Sergio Leone westerns are about violence.

Wrong.

When questions are hurled up at me from the college audiences I frequently burden with my presence, one of the most frequently asked is, "How did you get the idea for 'I Have No Mouth, and I Must Scream'?"

And when I respond, with absolute candor, that I had no idea what the story was about when I began writing it, I'm always treated to expressions ranging from disbelief to disbelief. Disbelief that such a "masterpiece" could emerge without the Author knowing what the hell he was doing. Disbelief that I'm telling the truth.

But that is exactly and precisely the truth.

There were two starting points. The first came from my friend Bill Rotsler, world-famous cartoonist, film maker, serious artist, world traveler, novelist, lover of women, *bon vivant* and ex-sculptor. Those who have been blessed with any space of time spent in William's company can verify that he is not only some of the very best hailfellow well-met associate with whom one can fritter away, golden time, but that he cannot go very long without doodling out some marvelous cartoons.

Not just the pudding-shaped little men and women engaged in sexual and pseudo-sexual shenanigans for which he is justly famous within a tiny circle of deranged devotees... but quicksketch of a philosophical and frequently heart-tugging seriousness. One of those little doodles, of a doll-like human being sitting and staring, with one of its facial features missing, slug-lined "I have no mouth and I must Scream," came into my possession some time during 1965. I saved it, and asked Bill if he minded if I used it as the title of a story that I might one day write. He said okay.

I put it aside. Then after a while had it mounted on a small square of black art-board and pinned it up near my typewriter. This was when I was living in the treehouse on Bushrod Lane in Los Angles.

A little later in the year I was visited by a then-San Diego-based artist named Dennis Smith. I had written several stories around Dennis's drawings— "Bright Eyes" and "Delusion for a Dragon-Slayer" are two that come immediately to mind. Periodically, Dennis would come up from San Diego to visit, and he'd bring along his folio. I would rifle through it fairly rapidly and select a few pieces I thought might spur the creation of a story. (I've enjoyed writing that way, around an already existent illustration, since my early pulp days when I had to write stories to fit atrocious covers on sf magazines.)

And I guess on Dennis's part it was partially flattery that a writer would use his work as impetus for new stories– Dennis was still an aspiring amateur in those days– and partially a hope that if I managed to sell the story,

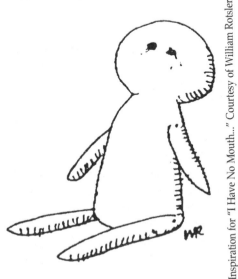

Inspiration for "I Have No Mouth..." Courtesy of William Rotsler

that I'd bludgeon the magazine into buying his art to accompany it. (I'd done it every time before so, he had every logical reason to assume it would always be the case. He was right; it was.)

From the folio that day in the summer of 1965, I pulled the Finlayesque pen-and-ink drawing I include here. That was the second starting point for "I Have No Mouth..." (Apparently, from a note written in the first paperback publication of the story, there was a second Smith drawing, similar to this, that I held onto. But it's long since gone.)

When I saw the drawing I made the instant connection between Rotsler's quote and the mouthless creature.

But that was all there was of the story. No plot, no theme, no idea of who or what or why.

But that's the way I like to write stories. If I must perforce now the ending of a story I'm creating, quite often I get bored with the writing... because I know

Inspiration for "I Have No Mouth..." Courtesy of Dennis Smith

how it's going to come out. And since I write to please and surprise myself, the thrill of writing a story that doesn't telegraph its punch-even to me-is one of the finer pleasures involved in the grueling act of fictioneering. Not to mention that *I'm* taken by surprise, the chances are good so will the reader.

(Parenthetically, I think this is as true a way of writing a story as heavily plotting one from the git-go. If one is creating characters that have verisimilitude, they will take the plot where *they* want it to go; and since human nature is as unpredictable as a topping fire, that direction will likely be a surprising, fresh way to go.)

So I sat down, rolled the paper into the Olympia Standard office machine I use, and began with the title "I Have No Mouth, and I Must Scream."

The first line wrote itself:

"Limp, the body of Gorrister hung from the pink palette..."

I had no idea who Gorrister was, nor why his body was hanging head-down, attached to that improbable pink palette by the sole of the right foot. But the first six pages went quickly. I stopped writing at the bottom of page six of the manuscript with the sentence "The pain shivered through my flesh." (Years later, going over the story, as I have many times to correct galleys for reprints of the work, I extended the sentence: "... shivered through my flesh like tinfoil on a tooth.")

Looking back at my original manuscript, I see that the idea creating time-breaks in the story by use of computer tape was an integral element from the very outset. On my yellow second-sheet copy of the original (that was in the days before I could afford a Xerox machine, when I used carbon and scuzzy $1.00-a-ream second-sheets for the files) I see that on page 2, after I had typed.

It was our one hundred and ninth year in the computer. He was speaking for all of us.

I typed an entire line of symbols stretching from margin to margin sequence from the keyboard:

QWERTYUIOPASDFGHJKLZXCVBNMQWERTYU

Sometime later, presumably right after I finished the story, I went back and, using cutouts from some kind of computer magazine I must have had lying around the tree house, I Scotch Taped colored overlays on those typed lines.

(When the story was finally submitted to *If: Worlds of Science Fiction* for publication, the use of computer tape for the break was ignored.

So were some of the breaks themselves, which altered the reading cadence, as far as I was concerned.)

The use of computer tape as an element in the story was more than a gimmick. During the middle sixties I was going through an extended period of annoyance at the physical limitations of the printed page. While I cannot deny that a writer should be able to create all the mood and superimposed precontinuum he needs for story simply by his/her skill with the English language, I think a writer who attempts to stretch the parameters of the fictive equation inevitably comes to a place where s/he rails at the conformity of simple symbols in neat parallel lines. I would feel presumptuous and foolish saying such a thing, were it not for those who have gone before me, who obviously felt the same: Laurence Sterne, James Joyce, Virginia Woolf, e.e. cummings, Alfred Bester, Gertrude Stein, Kenneth Patchen, Guillame Apollinaire-to name the most prominent lurking in memory.

My intent was to indicate that the story takes place actually and physically in the mind of the computer; that the characters are surrounded and dominated by the figment that AM has created as their world. One way to do this was to insinuate AM's running discourse with itself throughout the typographical makeup of the work.

Years later I was lucky enough to have several computer programmers offer to set the breaks with specific dialogue. They asked me what I would like AM to be saying in those breaks. I always *knew* what it was, but I'd never been able to get a publisher to lay out the money to have the tapes cut exactly.

I took the programmer/readers up on their offer. The computer tape time-breaks in the story now read:

"I think, therefore I AM" and "Cognito ergo sum."

Through the years, and through the many reprints of the story, I have had the most trouble with the *other* type-design elements, the "pillar of stainless steel bearing bright neon lettering." It was constructed to appear all on one page, as a physical representation of the pillar in the story, yet the ineptitude of copyeditors and typesetters prevented it from appearing that way until almost eight years after the story's first publication. (Yes, it was set in a column in *If,* but I had specified that the lines should fill, flush left and right, without a partial last line, what is called a "widow" in the industry... and if you check back to the March 1967 issue of *If* you'll see there's a pronounced "widow.")

These days I send along a separate design sheet with the preferred text for all reprints.

(Another aside. A friend named Burt Libe, who works with electronic gadgetry, has built for me a wonderful 16-byte binary counter with the words from AM's stainless steel pillar on the face. I have it plugged in near my desk. When it's flickering away, and I'm working, and strangers wander into the office and see that crazed screed about hating Humanity, they naturally draw the conclusion that I'm writing something ultimately detrimental to the well-being of the species. Oh well. Go explain your toys.)

I put the story aside after six pages. Other matters were pressing me hard at the time. Now the sequence of events return to Frederik Pohl's purview.

In 1965 I was still a relatively "uncelebrated" writer. And my attendance at the Milford (Pennsylvania) SF Writers Conference sponsored by Damon Knight, James Blish and Judith Merril was not a matter of very great concern for anyone but me. I have written elsewhere about my feelings of being a ratty poor relation, of having been "put in my place" years before by the legendary writers, and of having stayed away from Milford get-togethers for a long time while nurturing thoughts of revenge. I've written about that return visit elsewhere and, and of course, Damon has written elsewhere that I was making the whole thing up, that they'd taken me to their bosom immediately. Anyone who has ever met me knows the unlikely possibility of taking me to bosom at once. I rest my case as far as Damon's refutations go.

Anyhow. At the 1965 Milford do, I wanted to write a story for submission to the Giants in attendance at the workshop sessions that would blow them away. I wrote and put into the session a story called "'Repent, Harlequin!' Said the Ticktockman." Reception was mixed. I didn't really score a clean, clear victory of vengeance. Some of them liked it a lot, others thought it sucked.

But Fred Pohl came up on the weekend, from New York. The final day of every Milford soiree was a big party; and many East Coast editors sashayed up for the blowout.

When Fred appeared, I gave him the story to read.

He bought it for *Galaxy*. It appeared in the December 1965 issue. Without fanfare. (My name wasn't even on the cover. The names of C.C. MacApp, Norman Kagan, Algis Budrys, Willy Ley and Robert Silverberg were there, but not the kid.)

I'd had a couple of big fights with Fred about the title. He wanted to shorten it to "Repent, Harlequin!" I begged and pleaded and threatened, and he finally let it stand.

It won the very first Nebula award of the Science Fiction Writers of America in the short story category. It also won the Hugo presented by the 24th World Science Fiction Convention in Cleveland, September 1966.

They were my first two awards in the field.

Soon thereafter, Fred Pohl came through Los Angeles. He came to visit at the treehouse. I showed him the first six pages of "I Have No Mouth..." He liked the pages and said he'd insure the writing of the story with an advance payment. I needed the money.

But it wasn't until a month or so later when Fred called from New York to say that, seeing as how *If* had won the Hugo as the best sf magazine of the year, he had decided to put out a SPECIAL HUGO WINNERS ISSUE OF *If* in March of 1967, that I was goosed into going back to the story.

(It occurs to me I've hopelessly bollixed up my dates on this. Memory stirs like an old snake on a warm rock. How it *must* have happened was that Fred came to visit *before* the Cleveland WorldCon and I took the uncompleted manuscript-which had been in work for a year and a half-back East with me. I realize that to've been the progression because I worked on the story in hotel rooms at the Sheraton Cleveland during the convention and the Roger Smith Hotel in New York *after* Labor Day. So Fred must have approached me for the Hugo Winners Issue at Cleveland, after the Hugos were awarded. There now, I *think* that's correct.)

But the story was my second attempt at validating my existence to the cadre of Milford superstars who had–either actually or in my fantasies–treated me so offhandedly.

I returned to the 1966 Milford Conference with credentials. I was the first person ever to win a Hugo and a Nebula for the same story in the same year, and had won them for a story that had received a lukewarm reception the year before.

So I submitted "I Have No Mouth..." to the workshop sessions with a certain arrogance. I knew I had a hot item, and I was ready to eat up the slavish praise of those who, till that moment, had been my betters. This was my final bid to become one of their equals.

I should have known better. John Brunner and Virginia Kidd heaped praise on it; Jim Blish commended me, bless him; and the younger writers thought it was fine. But there were many of the old hands who put it down, found fault with it, excoriated me for excess, and blissfully I've forgotten who among them was the most vociferous. But it didn't really matter. The story appeared in that March 1967 Hugo winners issue of *If*, alongside Asimov, Zelazny, Niven, Budrys and Sprague de Camp.

And it won me my *second* Hugo.

The prophecy, a story written for a winners issue, itself won the award, fulfilling itself. As though it had all been planned, synchronism occurred, and the unbroken line of Milford conferences, Fred Pohl, "'Repent, Harlequin!',", the Hugo and Nebula, *Galaxy* and *If...* all of it fell into place and "I Have No Mouth..." published in magazine form in March, published as the title story of my collection in April, copped the silver rocket in September at the 26th WorldCon.

And though I railed at Fred for having published it sans the computer "talk-fields," though I screamed bloody murder at the Bowdlerizing of what Fred termed the "difficult sections" of the story (which he contended might offend the mothers of the young readers of *If*) nonetheless I am forced to give the Devil his due.

Fred Pohl, for all the aggravation he caused me through the years—we won't mention all the aggravation I've caused *him* through the years—was one of the few editors who gave me my head and let me write what I wanted to write in those days before the phrase "New Wave" started emerging from people's mouths. True, he told people I wanted him to publish "I Have No Mouth..." in four-colors, an error of memory he refuse to correct based on the manuscript coming to him with those colored cut-outs pasted to the pages; but for all his cantankerous, albeit friendly, canards he remain one of the truest judges of writing ability the field of imaginative literature has ever produced.

I cannot say that without his support "I Have No Mouth..." would not have been written; but it's certain that had Fred not championed those 6500 words I would not today be sitting here writing 30 to this memoir.

There is really not a great deal to be said about this story. It tells itself in straightaway terms, and makes its moral (I feel) somewhat heavily at the end. As I recall, I wrote it while I was in the US Army, stationed in Kentucky, and I'm not at all certain it was written for money. I think there was some of my horror at the "Southern intellect" hinted–at, in it. This may seem obscure, since this is a science fiction story about a circus and a group of telepaths, but for one who was, for many years, a Mickey Mouse parlor liberal, it was the first genuine stirrings of social conscience. We allow terrible things to happen, and turn our faces away in horror, but we never commit ourselves. Either we feel we are not in a position to do any good—ludicrous when exam- ined closely—or we cop–out intellectually, rationalizing the nature of the crime, and the nature of the struggle in the deepest, most esoteric, and most cheaply hypocritical terms. There is a song the kids in SNCC sing. It goes, "Which side are you on?" and that, friends, is where it's at. You're either for, or against. The time for fence–sitting is long past. Excuse the militancy. All this is from the viscera, and has very little to do with

BIG SAM WAS MY FRIEND

I guess working for a Teeper Circus ain't the quietest work in the Galaxy, but what the dickens, it's more than just a buck, and you see a lot of the settled worlds, and there's always enough quailette around to keep a guy happy, so why should I kick. By that I mean, so what if they *did* lynch my friend Big Sam out on Giuliu II? So what, you can always find another friend someplace around. But every time I start thinking that way, I kick myself mentally and say Johnny Lee, you got to stop passing Sam off like that. He was a good friend. He was a sick man, and he couldn't help what he did, but that's no call to be passin' him off so quick.

Then I'd start to remember the first time I'd ever seen Big Sam. That was outside Shreveport. Not the *old* Shreveport, but the one on Burris, with the green–sand hills just beyond in the dusk. We were featuring Dolly Blaze that time. She was a second stage pyrotic with a cute little trick of setting herself on fire, and what with her figure what it was, well, it wasn't much of a trick—even for a drum–banger like me—to kick up some pretty hot publicity about the circus.

It was the second show, and we'd packed the tent full—which wasn't odd, because two hundred Burrites, each as big as an elephant (and looking a little bit like elephants with those hose proboscises), crammed our pneumotent till there was hardly room for the hawkers to mill through—when I spotted him. It wasn't so strange to spot a Homebody from Earth on a Ridge world, what with the way we Earthmen move around, but there was something odd about *this* Homebody. Aside from the fact that he was close to seven feet tall.

It wasn't long till I spotted him as a teeper of some sort. At first, I figured him for a clairvoyant, but I could tell from the way he watched the acrobats (they were a pair of Hungarian floaters called the Spindotties, and the only way they could have fallen was to lose their teep powers of anti–grav altogether), the way he tensed up when they were making a catch, that he couldn't read the future. Then I figured him for an empath, and that would have been useless for the circus; except in an administrative capacity of course. To tell us when one of the performers was sick, or unhappy, or a bad crowd, or like that. But right then credits were tight and we couldn't afford an empath, so I counted him off. But as I watched him sitting there in the stands, between two big–as–houses Burrites sucking up pink lemonade from squeeze–bulbs, I discounted the empath angle, too.

I didn't realize he was a teleport till Fritz Bravery came on with his animal pack.

In our circus, we clear both side tings for the central circle, when a specialty act goes on. Then the fluorobands are jockeyed into position over the center ring, and the mini–tapes set their reaction music for all–bands. That way we draw attention to the big act only.

Fritz Bravery was an old–timer. He had been a lion–tamer in a German circus back Home, before teeping was understood, and the various types outlined. That was when Fritz had found out the reason he was so good with animals was that he was what the French had labeled *animaux–voyeur*. Which, in English, the way we accept it now, means he and the beasts think alike, and he suggests to them and like they just go through hoops if he thinks *jump through a hoop*.

But Fritz was also one of those harkeners after the old days. He thought show biz was dead, nothing but commercial and plebeian crap left. You know, one of those. And he had lost his wife Gert somewhere between Madison Square Plaza and Burris, and eventually the old joy juice had grabbed him.

That night old Fritz Bravery was juiced to the ears.

You could spot it the moment he got into the ring with the beasts. He was using three big Nubian lions and a puma and a dree and a sly-gor, those days. Plus one mean bitch of a black panther called Felice, the likes of which for downright cussedness I've never seen.

Old Fritz got with them, and he was shaky from the start. King Groth, who ran the show, looked at me, and I looked at him, and we both thought, *I hope to God Fritz can handle them tonight with his senses all fogged up like that*. But we didn't do anything, because Fritz always had his escape plate ready to lift him over their heads, if he got into trouble. And besides, it was *his* act, we had no right to cramp it before he'd shown his stuff.

But King murmured in my ear, "Better start looking around for a new cat man, Johnny. Fritz won't be good much longer." I nodded, and felt sort of sad, because Fritz was as good a cat man as we'd ever had with the circus.

The old man went around them, walking backward with his lektrowhip snapping and sparking sweetly, and for a while everything was fine. He even had the lions and the puma up in a tricky pyramid, with the black panther about to leap up the backs of the five lions, to take her place at the apex of the pyramid. He pulled off that number pretty well, though one of the lions stumbled as the pyramid was breaking up, and growled at him. We had grown to know the difference between a "show" growl—commanded mentally by Fritz—for fright effect in the act, and a real one. A real one free of Fritz's control. That was this last one. So we knew old Fritz was losing control.

We grew more alert as he herded the lions and the puma into the corner of the force–cage in which he performed his act. It was transparent around the four walls, but there nonetheless.

Then Fritz—ignoring Felice, who followed the other Earth–beasts—went to work on the dree. He got her to rotate on all sixteen, and hump, and then turn inside out, which is a pretty spectacular thing, considering a dree's technicolor innards. Then he got it to lift him on one appendage, and place him gently on another, all the way up the length of her body, from appendage to appendage.

Then he worked for a while with the slygor.

It was poisonous, so he donned gloves, and used the sonic–whistle on it alone. Since electricity did not affect it in any way. Even his work with the slygor was fair that night, and for a while we thought he would make it fine. I kept tossing this seven–foot Homebody in the stands a look from time to time, trying to decide what sort of a teep he was, but he was just watching the act, and smiling, and not doing a thing.

Then Fritz went to work on Felice.

She had been invershipped from Earth not more than three weeks before, and the trip through inverspace, coupled with her natural instinctive nastiness, and more than likely allied with some temperament quirk aggravated by the warping of the ship and its occupants through inverspace, had left her a jangle–nerved, heaped–up body of hate and fury. We had had several close calls with her nipping her feeder–robots, and I for one didn't like to see Old Fritz in there with her.

But he was determined to break her—showmanship and all that bushwah—so we let him go ahead. After all, he *did* have the escape plate there, which whisks him anti–gravitically over the heads of the animals, should there be trouble.

He picked up his lektrowhip, and moved in on Felice. She sat crouched back on her haunches, waiting him out. He stopped a foot from her, so close he could have stroked her sleek black fur. Then he did a double–movement crack–crack! with the lektrowhip, and caught her on the snout with a spark. Felice leaped.

At that precise instant, the most remarkable thing I've ever glommed in all my days as flack for a top, happened. I've never yet been able to figure it out—whether the beasts were actually in mental contact with one another, or it was just chance—but the puma got to its feet, and softly padded over to the escape plate . . . and sat down on it. The lions moved out, and positioned themselves around the force cage. Fritz was hemmed in completely. Then Felice began stalking him.

It was the most fascinating and horrifying thing I've ever seen. To witness that big cat, playing footsie with old Fritz. The tamer tried to control her, but even from where we were in the stands, we could see the sweat on his face, and the dark lines etched against the white of his face. He was scared; he had lost control of them completely. He knew he was dead.

Felice's eyes were two barbs, ready to impale poor old Fritz, and we were so stunned, it all happened so quickly, we just sat there and so help me God we just *watched!*

I felt like a Roman in the arena.

Felice crouched again, and the muscles in her black shoulders hunched and bunched and tensed, and she sprang full on old Fritz.

He fell down, and her crushing weight landed atop him, and her jaws opened wide, with yellow fangs straining yowpingly for Fritz Bravery's neck. Her head came up, and back, and her throat was stretched tight so the pulse of a blood vein could be seen, and then the head came down like the blade of a guillotine.

But Fritz wasn't there.

He was sitting up in the stands with the seven–foot Homebody.

That was when I knew. Hell, *anybody'd* be able to tell, by then. He was a teleport. The best kind—an outgoing teleport.

He had teeped Fritz out of the jaws of the black panther.

I looked at King Groth, who was looking from Felice to Fritz and back, not knowing I had already tagged the Homebody as a teeper, and there was amazement on his face.

"We got us a new star act, King," I said, slipping out of my seat. I cocked a thumb at Fritz, who was talking bewilderedly to the seven–foot Homebody. I started threading my way between the elephant–big Burrites, toward Fritz and his savior.

Behind me, I heard King Groth saying, "Go get 'im boy."

I got him.

Now I won't bother going into the year Big Sam spent with the circus. It was pretty routine. We covered the stardust route from Burris to Lyli A to Crown Colony to Peck's Orchard to MoultonX/11i11 (they have a treaty there with the natives, so long as they use both Homebody and native name for the planet) to Ringaling and right along the Ridge to the new cluster worlds of Dawnsa, Jowlak, Min, Thornwire and Giuliu II. That was where we lost Big Sam.

There on Giuliu II—where they lynched him.

But to understand what happened, *why* it happened, I'd better tell you about Big Sam. Not just that he was nearly seven feet tall, with a long, horsey face, and high cheekbones, and dark, sad blue eyes. But *about* him, what he was like.

And this is the best way to tell it:

Sam's act consisted of several parts. For instance, at the beginning, we turned off all the fluoro bands. Then three roustabots clanked out carrying this big pole in their metal arms. They would kick off the cover plate of the hole we had sunk in the floor of the arena or tent, and insert the pole in it, then clamp it so it was rigid.

Then one of the roustabots would switch on the torch–finger of his utility hand, and set fire to the pole. We had already doused it in oil, and the thing caught fire up its length, till there was a pillar of fire in the middle of the ring. It was a specially treated pole, and didn't really burn—though the fire on it was real enough—so we used the same pole over and over.

Then the ringmaster would swoop in on his plate, and his sonic voice would boom out at the audience, "Laydeez and Gentilmenn! I ddrawww your attenshuuun to the center rinnnng, where the Galaxy's most mystifying, most extraorrrrdinary artiste will perform for you. I am pppprowd to present: The Unbelievable Ugo!"

That was Sam.

Then the one spot would go on, like the eye of a god, and pick out Sam, striding across the plastidust (sawdust went out with the high cost of invershipping). He would be wearing skin–tight black clothing that accentuated his slim build, and high–topped black boots—very

soft and with two inch soles to make him seem even taller. And a black cape with a crimson lining. Helluva look, lemme tell ya.

He would advance to the center of the ring, just beside the burning pole, and raise his arms. A girl wearing spangles and not much else (that was Beatrice, whom I had been dating, when she wasn't on her iron filing kick—but that's another story, fortunately) would run out and take his cape, and Ugo, that's Sam, would turn and look at the pole for a long minute.

Then he would take a running leap, hit the pole and start to shinny up. Everyone would shriek. He was being burned to death. Then he was gone.

And a second later, he was at the top of the pole, on the little platform above the flames. Everyone was astonished. For some reason, they never realized he was a teleport. I guess there aren't many teleports around, and most people don't see them as flagrantly displaying their talents as Big Sam did. It's a recessive trait.

For a moment he would poise himself there on toetip, as the audios scirled their danger music on all–bands, and then as the drums rolled, Sam would do a neat swan dive off the platform. The shrieking would get even bigger then.

He would turn a gainer, a flip, a half–gainer and then—just as it seemed he was about to smash full force into the ground—he disappeared and reappeared standing lightly on the balls of his feet, in the same position he had been when he started—his arms widespread over his head, an enigmatic grin splitting his craggy features.

That was the first part of his act. The applause was always deafening. (And we never had to modify it by taped responses, either, isn't that beyond belief?)

To see an almost certain horrible death—you know how crowds all sit on the edge of their seats, *praying* subconsciously for a spectacular accident—and then to be whisked away from it so suddenly—brought to the edge of tragedy, and then to have their better natures win out, showing them how much nicer they always *knew* they were—that was the supreme thrill.

But it was merely a beginning.

Then Ugo–Sam did juggling—magnificent high–flown juggling with hundreds of knives, and fireballs, and even thousand–pound weights—moving them all by teleportation. Then he wrestled with the bear, slipping out of the most fearsome grips, as easily as a greased fish. Then came the tennis match he played with himself. (He beat himself in straight sets.)

His act was sensational. For on many of the outer Ridge worlds, they had had little or no truck with teleports. By the Service system for teeps, each of the categories had to send representative members to the Ridge worlds to serve tours, to spread Homebody technology and advantages around, but there were so few teleports, they had been rarely seen.

So Big Sam was a novelty. And as such, he dragged the credits for us. I played him big.

But there was more to Sam than just the tricks.

We used to sit alone at night under a saffron sky, or a mauve sky or an ebony sky, and talk. I liked talking to him, because he wasn't dumb, like most of the washed–up and used–up carny creeps we had with us. He had been an educated man, that was obvious, and there was a deep, infinite sadness about him that sometimes made me want to cry, just talking to him there.

I remember the night I found out how sick Big Sam really was. That was on Rorespokine I, a little plug of a world by all rights we should have avoided; but a combination of low money for paychecks, repair work for the ships, and general all–around lethargy, had set us down on that whistle stop for a three–week set.

Mostly, we just puttered around and killed time resting up till the big six month tour on Giuliu II.

That night, Big Sam and I lay back with our heads on grassy mounds, staring up at the night that was deep blue with the stars ticking away eternity over us. I looked over at the rough topography of his face, and asked him, "Sam, what the hell is a guy like you doing out on the fly like this?"

His face tightened all over. It was so odd, the way he looked. So tight, like my question had sucked all the life from him.

"I'm looking for a dead girl, JohnnyLee." He always pronounced my name as though it were one word only. His answer didn't sink in for a second.

I didn't want to push, but I felt somehow this was the first opening–up he had ever given me.

"Oh? How'd that happen?"

"She died a long time ago, Johnny. A long time ago."

His eyes closed. He no longer saw the stars.

"She was just a girl, Johnny. Just another girl, and I guess I was more in love with the idea of love, than with her."

I didn't say a word. For a long time, neither did he. Then, when I was starting to fall asleep, and thought he already had, he went on: "Her name was Claire. Nothing very pretentious about her, so simple and clean. I wanted very much to marry her, I don't know why, we were nothing alike. Then one day we were walking, and I don't know what it was—just something, you know—and I teleported away from her. Half a block away. I didn't know then, quite, what I could do. I had never teleported in front of Claire. I suppose it was a shock to her. She was a No–Talent, and it must have shocked her. I could see she was repulsed by the idea of it."

"I'd, I'd been . . . sleeping with her, Johnny, and I guess it was pretty foreign. Like finding out the guy you'd been making love to was an android or some–such. She ran away. I was so shocked at her attitude, I just didn't follow her.

"Then I heard a screech and she screamed, and I teleported to the source of the scream, and she'd been hit by a truck, trying to cross the street. Oh, it wasn't my fault, nothing like that, and no guilt complex or anything, but—well, you know, I had to get away from things. So I took to the fly. Just like that."

He was finished. I said, "Just like that. You ever goin' back, Sam?"

He shook his head. "I don't suppose so. I'll find her someday."

I said, "Huh?"

He glanced over, and there was a hurt in his eyes. "Yeah, I suppose I never told you this, probably think it's a crazy idea; everyone else does. She's in Heaven."

"Nothing crazy about that, Sam," I said, big magnanimous that I was.

"Heaven is out here somewhere."

That stopped it. I was back to, "Huh?"

He nodded again. "Out here, on one of these, is Heaven. That's where she is. I'll find her." He waved at the stars overhead. I followed his arm. Up here? Heaven? On an alien world? I didn't say anything.

"Crazy?"

"No, I don't suppose it's any crazier than any other idea of Heaven or Hell," I replied soberly. It gave me the creeps, frankly.

"I'll find her."

"I sure hope so, Sam. I sure hope so."

He fell asleep before I did. Who could sleep with something like that to scare the crap out of you?

We hit Giuliu II on a Thursday, and by the following Friday a week, we had a command performance scheduled for the Giuliun royalty. It was a wonderful deal; once we had performed and pleased the court, our success on Giuliu II was assured. Because they had a real Monarchy Plus set up on that world. And if the court liked us, the high glub–glub or whatever the hell they called the king, would send out a proclamation ordering all his subjects to attend or suffer some penalty. So we'd be all set.

We ran through the acts, in the palace, which was a great mansion, twice as big as our pneumotent, and I've got to admit, even washed-out Dolly Blaze and Fritz Bravery and the rest were magnificent. But, of course, Sam stole the show. They had never seen a teleport on Giuliu II, and Sam was at his sparklingest best. He was more daring and unusual than ever. There was even a trick with Felice that had everyone gasping and finally chuckling.

When it was over, the king and his court invited us to a huge banquet, and ceremonial party. It was the greatest. They had huge platters of fried and braised meats, bowls of planetary fruits, tankards of ales and liqueurs that were direct lineal descendants of ambrosia. It was the greatest.

Then they brought on the dancing girls, and they were even better. I spotted one smooth–limbed little number I decided to approach with dalliance in mind, after everyone had settled down a little. The

Giuliuns were Homebody type right down to their navels, and I wasn't worried about picking up any alien equivalents of VD. Besides, she had the cutest little po–po I'd seen in months. Beatrice, the girl who assisted Sam, and who I had been shacking with, was eyeing me, and eyeing a handsome brute, all tanned and wearing bronze armor, who was guarding one of the big doors. I decided to let her cheat on me, thus leaving the road clear for the little dancer.

The party was well under way, when the king stood up and made some big deal announcement about us being just in time to see the Sacred Virgin Ceremony of Giuliu II, which occurred but once every twenty–five years. He even hinted it had been moved up a few weeks to accommodate us in this hour of circus triumph. We all applauded, and watched as they set up a high platform made of ever–smaller gold risers. It was quite a thrill.

We were all gathered around at the one end of the ceremonial hall, with the pyramid of risers at the other. We weren't interested, in the least, about this ceremony; but to be polite we watched as they set up some sort of chopping block affair, and put two burning braziers beside the block.

It was getting more interesting by the moment. While most of the circus folk were still gorging themselves on the foods and fruits overflowing the table, Sam and I turned full around to watch this. I heard him mumble something about picturesque native ceremonies, and nodded my head.

The king signaled to one of his bully–boys, and the bully–boy swung a long–handled clapper at a tapestry hanging from floor to ceiling beside him. They must have had a gong concealed behind it, because the sound almost deafened me.

Then the king—of his title I'm not sure, but his rank was obvious—spoke for a few minutes on the history and traditions of the Sacred Virgin Ceremony. We didn't really listen too closely, mainly because he was speaking in similes and the noise from the crowd around us drowned him half out.

But in a little while we got the impression this was very important stuff to the Giuliuns, and when the king clapped his hands, we turned to the gang, and tried to get them to shut up. Those slobs would rather eat than think.

They didn't shut up till the gong sounded again, but when the gray–hooded man with the gigantic meat cleaver brought the pretty blonde girl out onto the platform, they all signed off like we'd cut their vocal cords.

She was a magnificently beautiful creature. Her hair was long and blonde, and her body was full and straight. Her eyes the deepest and most lustrous brown I've ever seen.

The executioner—hell yes! that's what he was—helped her over to the block, and her face was very calm. Calm, it seemed, the way someone's face would be if they were dying of cancer, and knew they could do nothing about it. But this young girl wasn't dying of cancer; she was about to have that gray–hooded man chop off her head.

It was apparent, that was what was about to happen.

A sacrificial ceremony.

The hooded man helped her to kneel before the block, and she lay her head in the notch. The executioner pulled her hair away from her neck, gently, and laid it over her left shoulder in a long blonde streamer.

Then he tested his hatchet's edge, and stepped back. He planted his feet wide apart, and swung the axe up. Everyone screamed, and it sounded like a million buzz–saws. Before anyone could do anything, the executioner brought the axe down almost touching her neck, to get the proper placement for the real swing.

That was when I heard Sam's muted gurgle. He had been mumbling, there beside me, for over a minute, and I hadn't realized it, I was so engrossed in watching the tableau on the chopping block. Then I heard him mutter, "Claire!"

And I knew there was going to be trouble.

I saw him stand up, out of the corner of my eye, and as the executioner swung the axe up in a two–handed whirl, Sam disappeared from beside me, and the next instant, before the blade had a chance to fall on that lovely neck, he was there. His arm snaked around the gray–hooded man's neck, and his hand shot out to catch the descending handle of the axe.

He wrenched the death tool from the man's hand, and threw it with a spinning clatter to the floor of the chamber far below the pyramid. Then his fist came back and caught the hatchetman across his hidden face. The executioner stumbled, and Sam doubled him over with a belly–blow that made the face behind the gray hood scream. Sam straightened him with a right to the tip of the jaw, and the hatchetman went caroming off the pyramid. He landed with a sick thump.

The king was on his feet, livid with rage, and the court was scream-ing, "Profanity! Outrage! Transgression!" The king clapped his hands, and a dozen of the tanned bully–boys (one of whom was the hawg Beatrice had been ogling) raced onto the pyramid and grabbed Sam around the waist, the neck, the legs and of course he teleported out of their grip. He was back beside me. The king was leaping up and down, screeching at the top of his lungs, to *get* that man. Sam stood impassively, waiting. Then King Groth walked over, and said, "Stand still, Sam. Let' s find out how much damage you've done."

He went to talk to the other king. Groth was a sharp operator, and if anyone could pour oil on the waters, it was him. We watched as he talked to the king, who was getting more furious and apoplectic by the moment.

"Sam, Sam," I said quietly, "why did you do it? For Christ's sake, *why?*"

He looked at me, and said, "This isn't much like Heaven, is it." Then I knew he had found Claire.

The blonde girl still kneeled beside the chopping block. She had not moved, except to raise her head from the notch.

King Groth came back, and his face was gray.

"Sam, they say you have to die."

Big Sam looked at him, and didn't say a word. I don't think he cared, really.

"Look, Sam, we're going to fight this. They can't do it to a Homebody. We can fight it, don't worry."

The king rushed over, and started to screech something. "Listen," I piped in, just to stop him, "he is a sick man, he didn't know what he was doing. You have to remember he knows nothing of your local customs."

It didn't make a bit of difference. "He must die. That is the reward for interrupting the Sacred Virgin Ceremony."

We argued and hassled and made a big stink out of it, and I think the only reason we all didn't gallop out of there and pull up stakes was that we were afraid we'd *all* be held and executed. And Big Sam was the only teleport in the crowd. And there was something else; something I'm afraid and ashamed, even today, to say.

I think we were all afraid of losing the business.

That's right. Pretty disgusting, ain't it? We could have set Dolly Blaze to burning the joint, and we could have escaped. We could have done at least a hundred things to distract the Giuliuns. But we were afraid we'd lose the business, and we were almost willing to let the man die for that.

Finally, though, the king said: "We must leave it to the Sacred Virgin, then. Let her decision be the one."

That sat okay with us—we wanted a way out so bad then it didn't matter—and we all looked at Sam. Softly, the hurt came back into his eyes, and a softness surrounded his mouth, and he nodded. "That's fine," he said simply.

We all walked up to the pyramid, and looked at her. She was very clean and simple looking. Just the way I'd imagine Sam's Claire might have looked. We all stared at her, and with a sneer, she snarled, "Let him die!"

And that was that.

They took him up to the block, and they removed her, and they shoved Sam's head into the notch. Then someone made the motion that he be hung, because the block was reserved for the Sacred Virgin. So they strung up a fiber rope—right there in that beautiful hall—and they put it around Sam's neck, and ten men got on the other end of the rope that hung over a beam from above.

And we just watched. Can you understand that? We just stood there and watched as Sam was prepared for hanging. I tried to stop them, finally. I suppose I came out of my trance. "Wait, you can't do this!" But King Groth and two of the performers grabbed me by the arms, and held me.

"This is their world, Johnny, let them do what they have to do."

And Sam looked at me, and I could see in his eyes that it didn't matter to him. It was the same hurt, all over again. He had been wrong; he *did* have a hag riding him about Claire's death. This was one way to clear it off.

They yanked on the rope, and Sam went up.

He hardly twisted or kicked or twitched.

I couldn't watch.

Because there were a couple of things that made me ill way deep inside. The first was knowing King Groth and the circus and even myself, had sacrificed this nice, quiet guy with a problem, for the sake of a credit. And the other thing, the thing that really stopped us from trying to help him, I think, was that Sam wanted to die. He could have teeped out of that noose at any moment, but he didn't. He let them lynch him. He had squared away with Claire.

We finished our tour on Giuliu II. Sam had been right: it wasn't much like Heaven.

I used to think I was ugly. Well, it wasn't exactly a vagrant whim on my part; I really was awfully miserable–looking. Short, pale, scrawny, braces, glasses, I sucked my thumb, I had pimples. Yechhh. With the exception of Helen Ralph and Jean Bittner in Painesville, when we were all too young to know what "infant sexuality" was all about, I never even kissed a girl till I was nineteen. I have tried to make up for it since then. Now, today, I am able to get across a mystic impression that I am a handsome devil. It is, of course, an illusion. For those of you out there in paperbackland who also feel grotty, I will pass along my secret. The emmis, the truth, pay attention. Think pretty. Now if you'd rather have some charlatan fleece you of a couple of grand with beauty treatments or plastic surgery or social dancing or how to speak grammatical Urdu, then go ahead, get took. But if you want the easiest way to do it, just heed those two words. Think pretty. Conceive of yourself as dashing, debonair, cool, filled with panache and aplomb. And soon the aura spreads out from inside you, and all them tender juicy items are pausing to reconsider you. Because, friends and neighbors, we live in a Time of Beautiful People. Gorgeous is revered. We can't stand anything even remotely ordinary; it has to be young and lovely. So you are not where it's at, if you aren't pretty. The trend is up, and it's getting worse. We spend billions more on cosmetics each year than education, and if it continues to spiral, soon enough we will come to a time when we may contemplate

EYES OF DUST

"In the kingdom of the blind, a one–eyed man is God." Contrariwise, in a world of absolute beauty, who labels ugliness?

It was inevitable they should marry. She with the mole on her right cheek, he blind in the presence of light. There should have been no reason for tolerating them on Topaz; on a world dedicated to beauty, imperfection could not be endured. Yet, they lived, and were avoided, and mated. As it should have been. Beauty seeks its level, as does ugliness. As do pariahs.

So they were married, and they managed to live, and soon, she was with child.

The terrible thing began.

The city of Light on the planet Topaz rose five hundred feet into the pearl sky. Its towers glowed with an aura imprisoned in the matter itself. All pastels: all blues and pinks and soft greens, that blended into one blinding impression of flow and swirl. The towers were of three heights. Sweeping giants that rose five hundred feet to the fraction of an inch; medium–sized towers that were mere pauses at three hundred feet, before the giants hurled past them; and midget towers, delicate and impertinent in their hundred–foot rise.

Glistening, diving, then arching in to a hold at another tower, the flying bridges and roadways were marvels of construction. At the various levels, clear layers of substance provided risers and dividers, giving the city the look of a fairy empire, set away from an ugly world, swathed in its own beauty.

And the people.

Each man, woman, child was a note in a great symphony of perfection. Both simplicity and flamboyance were there, but so inter-

66

mingled and integrated that nowhere could coarseness be discerned. Their faces were neither blank nor vapid. They held beauty in their eyes, and in the clearness of their complexions, and the rhythm of their stride.

There was nothing but beauty on Topaz. In the city of Light there was nothing but the glorious presentation of perfection and elegance. It was a vital culture, rich in thought, complex in design, but dedicated to the beauty of life, and the reflection of that beauty in all things material.

The blind man and his wife, the moley woman, lived in the small units outside the city, where the farmers tilled their symmetrical fields with equipment that was handsome in its construction, efficient in its operation.

They lived in a split–level home that boasted all modern robotic conveniences. The lights dimmed or shone according to palmed instructions; heat radiated from those walls at the touch of a stud; food was prepared by fail–safe robochefs; snits hummed from wall–cubbies to clean up instantly.

In the machine cellar, where the servomechanisms were housed, where the nerve center of the house was located, the blind man and the moley woman had constructed an extra room, set off from the light, for a special purpose. In the room, soft walls shrouded sound, protected the inhabitant from outside distractions. In the room, no light penetrated, and the bed was a pallet of downiness.

The inhabitant was Person.

Person, for no other name had ever been given him. Not like the blind man, who was Broomall, or the moley woman, who was Ordak. They had names, for they went abroad onto Topaz occasionally, and had to deal with others. But no such intercourse was practiced by Person. He never saw the light, and he never strolled, for the room was his home, and his parents had insured he would never venture from it.

In the machine cellar of the split–level out beyond the city of Light, Person sat in stolid silence, hands folded delicately in his lap, feet turned inward and at rest.

Eyes of dust filled with—not quite?—colors that moved.

Person could not have been endured on Topaz. On a world of beauty, all beauty, ugliness was a known and despised factor. Broomall and

Ordak were malformed . . . a mole and blindness . . . but they had been in the community long, and they were intelligent enough to keep to themselves. But their offspring was another matter.

With eyes of dust, who could tolerate such a thing?

Broomall unpalmed the door, and entered.

"Father . . . " Person murmured in a tongue as sweet as brook water, tones like butterflies' wings.

"Yes. How are you today? Have you had another vision?"

Person nodded, his gray sockets turning toward the blind man. "It came earlier, Father. Deepest black, with bright shoots of red thrusting up. It reminded me of the mouth of a volcano, Father."

The blind man felt his way to the pallet, lowered his body, and shook his head slowly. "But you have never seen a volcano, my son."

Person took a step away from the wall, and his great hands hung loosely below his knees. "I know."

"Then, how—"

"The way I saw the gulls dipping over the green spit of land. The way I saw the deep river of orange mud that bubbled its way to the swamp. It is all one, Father. I see."

The blind man shook his head in bewilderment. There were answers here; to questions he had never asked.

"Where is Mother? She has not been to see me in several times."

The blind man sighed. "She must work, Son, if we wish to fill up our food bins. She has taken labor in the wafting center."

"Ah." Person conjured up a vision of the sense centers, where smells and sounds and feelings of beauty were poured out on the air of Topaz, for the inhabitants to enjoy. "She must like it there. So near to the scent of gardenias."

"She says it's a job."

Person nodded. His great head bowed slightly, and pits of shadow marked his eyes of grayness.

"Is there anything you want?"

Person slid down the wall, into the cool darkness, and answered softly, for he knew his father was without sight, even without the sight *he* possessed. "No, Father. I lack for nothing. I have my meal cakes and my ale. I have my shadows and my colors. And there is the smell of time passing. I need nothing more."

"How strange you are, my son," the blind man said. Person gave a soft musky chuckle of amusement.

"How strange I am indeed, Father."

The blind man got slowly to his feet, the bones of his legs cracking barely. "Soon, my son," he said finally.

"Go sweetly, my father," Person said, using the words of the people of Topaz.

"Stay softly," replied his father, traditionally.

Then he went out, carefully palm–locking the door and setting it to a fresh combination. Caution could not be too deep in this matter. Twenty years had shown that. Twenty years, during which time their son had remained alive, to roam at will in his world of strange blind–sight.

The blind man climbed the ramp to the living floor, and sat cross–legged on his low platform, sending soft pipings flickering from a helix–shaped flute.

He played without break for some time, until the porter glowed pink and Ordak took form in the bowl.

"Wheeew!" She stepped out of the bowl and sank onto a nest of foamettes. "What a day. If I never smell another gardenia, it'll be too soon. Good evening, dear. How was he today?"

The blind man laid aside his flute, and extended his arms to the woman. He took her into their enfolding circle and held her dark hair against his neck. His answer was a grunt. She understood.

"How will it be, Broomall? Tell me."

He put her from him gently, and sighed. "Ordak, how can I say it'll be good, when it gets worse each day? You know he can't go out, and you know we must live here . . . they would never tolerate him outside, even to the spaceport and off. We're trapped here, my darling."

She stood up and smoothed down the front of her sweepspun tunic and skirt. Her hair was coiffed in such a way that the mole on her right cheek was covered. They knew of her deformity, of course, but not seeing it made it easier for them.

She was standing there, wondering what would come from the future, her blind husband at her feet, when the future dropped from the sky.

As she stood there, silent, and wondering, the force–bead drive of a cross–continent copter ruptured and the ponderous vehicle plunged down from its cruising level at twenty–five hundred feet. It fell two hundred yards from the split–level, demolishing the aboveground sections of the home without warning. Only the machine cellar was saved by a fluke of impact; saved for the searchmecks and analyzers that came later, to estimate the damage, and to extricate those left alive.

Aboveground, no one was left alive. The last two known imperfects on Topaz had gone to a companionable rest; where beauty and ugliness had no meaning.

But belowground . . .

The terrible thing began in earnest. What had lain in wait for twenty years, now snarled, leaped, and threw itself at the throat of beauty on Topaz.

They found him meditating.

They came down through the rubble with forcepak beams that melted the twisted metal and fused plastic into solid, attractive walls of pastel, between which they picked their delicate way. When they came to the secret room—whose door was not in the least pleasing to the eye—they stopped, perplexed, and considered what to do.

There were three of them, handsome men in the extreme. One was blond, with wide–set blue eyes and the air of an executive. He carried himself within his gold and copper–thread tunic with the calm assurance of a man who knows he is competent and handsome. In the extreme. The second was only a few inches shorter than the first man's six feet, and his dark, tightly–curled head of hair swooped delicately down across a sculpted white forehead. He gave an immediate impression of Adonis–like proportions.

The third man was the classic Greek ideal of virility and competence. His deep–set gray eyes snapped back and forth with authority and compassion. His walk was the walk of the legionnaire, his speech the measured cadence of the wise man. He would never go bald, his smile would never fade.

"I've never seen anything like this, before," said the curly–haired analyzer, whose name was Roul.

"This isn't standard in machine cellars, is it?" asked the leader, whose name was Prathe.

The third man, Hold, shook his head. "No, and I must admit it's an unpleasant arrangement. Unsprayed. Crude." He gave a soft shudder.

"Well, let's open it," suggested Prathe, hefting his forcepak.

The other two did not answer, and that was a perfect sign of agreement, so he applied the beam. A wide arc of fruit–green streamed out and washed the door. In a few seconds it had fused along the sides, and run together in excellent symmetry. They stared through into the thrusting darkness.

They found him meditating.

When first the light filtered through from behind them, they could not discern that it was human. It was a gray heap hulked close to the angle of floor and wall, its great head hung down, and hands turned into the lap.

Then, as the particulars became clear, each man in turn drew a shocked breath. Pathe was first into the room, and his voice was an *almost*–unpleasant mixture of wonder and revulsion.

Roul followed, and as the form of Person grew specific, he uttered a round, pear–shaped, then suddenly, shattered cry of terror. "How vile!" And his face was unhandsome. In the extreme.

Hold shone his light down into the corner, and away as quickly. In its wild travels, the beam covered the room completely: pallet, bare walls, small dish with gruel still in it, mat on the floor. Then back to Person again, but this time, the pool of brilliance was directed at the floor and the edge of the Person's buttocks, so the full light did not fall on that face—Oh that face!

The great head with its high unkempt crown of nearly white hair . . . spread out and in two huge tufts at either temple. The heavy–jowled face, with the mouth that was a wicked, slanting slash through the pale white flesh. The ears that hugged close and round to the head.

Then the eyes . . .

The eyes of dust . . .

Two deep–nested pockets, where gray swirled. The gray of decaying bodies. The gray of storm clouds. The gray of feelings most unhappy, and of death. The eyes that seemed to see so deeply, yet could see nothing. Ugly eyes.

They raised their forcepaks, and Person stirred.

First there was light, and then there was no–light. First there was heat, and then there was no–heat. And —

First there was love, and then there was no–love. But in its place did not come the absence of love, the emptiness that the going of light and heat had left. Another moved in to take its place.

In its place came hate.

Much later, when the suns had set, and the moons had come up to mourn balefully in silence over the world of beauty, Topaz, others came. They found the three bodies, so ugly in death, so unhandsome in crushed and battered death.

Then they took him. They took him out, saying, "All this, all this." And there was such revulsion and such cursing and hatred for him. He was anathema. Pariah! He was ugliness amidst beauty.

"What will we do with him? How can we kill him?"

Then one came forward. A poet whose meters were correct, whose images were gorgeous. He was slim and well–mannered and it fell to him to envision the right way of it. To create beauty from ugliness, good from evil.

So they erected a straight silver pillar, and it rose shining and true toward the four moons, and they tied him to it, and set the faggots about. Then they lit him and watched him burn.

But Person had eyes of dust, and the eyes of dust saw what could not be seen, and the soul within was the sweet soul of the visionary.

He had the audacity to weep and cry as he burned, wailing, "Do not kill me! There is so much for me to see, so much I do not know!" He sobbed for the knowledge and visions he would never glimpse.

And it was good. The fire was beauty. (If only he had been wise enough not to scream!)

When the ashes settled, they were melted, and there was a perfect pool of lustreless silver where the pillar and Person had been.

It was beauty, as all was beauty.

And there were none who would dispute it: everything was beauty on Topaz now, they said. Beauty and peace.

But the night sky rang with the stifled and fading shrieks that would never entirely pass. And as the clouds passed before two of the moons, looking so much like the eyes of dust, it was clear that Topaz had cursed itself with ugliness.

The pastel towers were hideousness imprisoned in crystal, the now clumsily arching bridges were offensive to the sight, and even the very air, the very sweet and moist air, had turned foul and rancid.

To anyone who was weak and would admit it, it was obvious: eyes of dust could never be closed.

Any number of followers of my work have asked me with creased brows, why I chose to have so many of my stories during the past three years appear in a "girlie" magazine called Knight. They feel, bless 'em, that anything I write should be first exposed in, maybe the Saturday Review or Harper's or Evergreen Review. Well, by way of answering them, consider: Knight does not edit my stories but prints them untouched as I submit them; they get Leo and Diane Dillon (my friends and the cover artists of the original edition of this volume) to do the illustrations; then pay me much less than many other markets, but very much a top dollar as far as their own rates are concerned; they let me experiment. Also consider, the previously–noted magazines seldom use science fiction, and when they do, it is of a certain stripe. It has been my contention for several years, that science fiction and the mainstream are no longer distinctly separate branches of the literary swim. Science fiction has been integrated in many ways—some valid and worthwhile, some hideously corrupted and sterile. But the melding of the two forms seems to me of prime importance for the continued virility and growth of both. Vonnegut has showed us the way. And Anthony Burgess. And John Hersey in The Child Buyer; and Only Lovers Left Alive, flawed as it was; and Bernard Wolfe in Limbo; and there are others. One such minor attempt to meet this challenge, as I was allowed to face it in the pages of Knight, is the character study called

WORLD OF THE MYTH

Dragon's breath! Fire split up the night sky; and out of the darkness silence a screaming erupted across the blue–black heavens. From the center of the fire–lick a speck of silver and gray careered across the horizon, finally losing its sidewise drive, and began to fall. A stone in the sky.

Sliding down the backdrop of the billion stars, the speck hurtled toward the dark world below, spewing fire and flowers of black smoke, oily smoke, from its drive tubes. It dropped as though discarded by some God from His sky.

It fell in swooping arcs, insanely, swinging back and forth across the silent night as though whoever piloted it was frantically trying to keep its leading saucer–edge up.

It came down in one last swooping glide and roared over the edge of jungle that stretched nearly to the golden sea. The ship came down in the dunes, plowing a long, canary–colored furrow in the sand, and split like a ripe pod. A flare of red spat up from the ruptured tubes in one last gasp of power, but no explosion followed it.

There was the tiny sound of metal popping, crackling, cooling. Then silence as the ship lay where it had crashed, crumpled into a weird shape, one fin thrown up like a dislocated arm; it lay spent and useless, sent to the ground.

The sea rolled up; the dunes hummed emptily, softly; the jungle screamed; but nothing came near the ship to disturb its slovenly grave.

Sunlight shafted through a great rent in the hull, sending a swath of gold across Cornfeld's forehead and eyes. He lay unmoving for a time, then as the heat reached him, he stirred in his sleep–after–

unconsciousness and threw an arm across his eyes. For a while longer he lay that way, till the heat grew oppressive; then he stirred. And began to move.

He made his way across the rubble of the plot–cabin and without thought to Iris Crosse or even Rennert, he stopped, on hands and knees, head hanging down, and drew great deep breaths. Thoughts began to patter along the track of his mind . . . alive . . . the crash . . . he was alive . . . that was important . . . the other two were in here . . . perhaps alive, perhaps not . . . but *he* was alive . . .

Consciousness came back fully now, and he stood up with unsteadiness. He pulled his ripped shirt loose from his jump–slacks and unsealed the front, He tossed the rag from him, and filled his lungs with air. Thank God. Alive!

He took three steps, trying to walk, staggered forward, and fell heavily on his side.

He lay that way for a few minutes, then stumbled to his feet.

He found Iris Crosse in her cabin, pinned beneath a wall cabinet that had broken free. Both her legs were crushed, but she was alive; she didn't seem to be bleeding internally. He managed to pull her out, and he carried her so light in his arms, back down the crazily–tilted corridor, to the rip in the ship's skin.

He laid her down gently on the soft yellow sand, in the deepest part of the shadow of the fin. Then he looked down at her. Her face, even in unconsciousness, held the same willful power that had helped wreck the ship. If she had not had the fight with Rennert and used her boot on him, he would not have fallen against the console and dumped the pile rods, causing the explosion.

It had been merely chance that they had fallen to this planet. Had the accident occurred further out, they would have gone off into the deeps, forever—or until the tubes had split the ship with their fury. Had they been closer, he would not have been able to plow in with a dead console.

A faint stirring in the golden sand drew his attention across the dunes, almost to the edge of the lush jungle. Only heat–dancers. He turned away.

She was looking at him. There was glaze over her dark, piercing eyes, but she was looking at him. He saw her mouth work, and it looked so odd, for her lipstick had smeared across her mouth, onto one cheek. Her tongue came out and touched her lips, and then—in a chain reaction that began with the eyes widening—her face masked over with an expression of pain and torture. "No! W–Wayne . . . don't . . . stop, Wayne! I, no, stop . . . *you!*" And she fainted again.

Cornfeld sat down heavily in the sand, and his hands went to his long brown hair absently. He knew what fear had possessed her, and again he heard the sounds and saw the sights of the night Wayne Rennert had raped the woman.

Five months out in a Surveyship was a long time, but there had been no call for it, no need for it, no explanation. Rennert was a peculiar person; amoral more than immoral.

He dragged his thoughts away from the act as it had happened, and tried to slip himself into a scheme of reality for the situation at hand.

They were down on an alien planet, without any help, and with Rennert dead . . . he stopped . . . dead? *Was* Rennert dead? He had not, for an instant, considered it any other way. Cornfeld's mouth went very dry; he realized he had *wanted* Rennert to be dead. But was he? Was it the situation he desired: alone on a desert island with Iris, without the deep, collie–brown eyes and wavy hair of Rennert always about? Was that what he had wanted . . . and was that the way it had turned out?

He got to his feet, feeling the sun beat down across his shoulders as he rose out of the tail fin's shadowy cool. Once more he crawled into the ship, and tacked along its battered insides, searching for the body.

There was no one in Rennert's stateroom. There was no one in the galley, and no one anywhere else in the plot room or the corridors.

He looked up at the downladder. It had been torn in half like a streamer of confetti, halfway down from its ceiling egress. In flight, the ladder lay on the floor, and the crew stepped over it when going from the lower half of the ship to the upper. Planetside, it ran up and down through the vessel, and with it broken off, gaining access to the other half of the saucer–shaped vessel was a difficult task.

He crawled back out through the rent in the hull, and did a careful tour of the ship. The saucer had plowed in snout first, leading edge first. The tail was in the air. The ship looked like a discus, imbedded in sand. In effect, it was. But whatever the comparisons, the lower half of the ship was in the air, and the upper section was thrust deep into the planet's soil.

76

Cornfeld went back inside. Rennert—if he was alive—was still up there in the sky–aimed half, and did he want to go get him? Did he want to find out if the man was alive, or did he want to balm his guilt with the thought Rennert had perished in the crash?

But what if he had been in the stores room, or the collar between sections? Lying there, needing help?

No! The answer came so distinctly, he was amazed to find himself stacking fallen lockers and equipment, in an effort to reach the snapped–off ladder. If he hated Rennert, why was he doing this? *Let him lie there!* He piled the debris higher.

From somewhere above came the sound of metal straining, rasping along metal. And bits of wall–surfacing material fell from the opening above. He paused in his efforts, his face suddenly still, and looked up. The sound did not come again. Was it the ship settling? Or something else?

After a moment, he dragged a console attachment to the tower of rubble, and heaved it up with difficulty, feeling every bruised bone in his chest and back. He supported himself on a dangling strut, hanging like a silver snake from the ceiling, and climbed to the summit of the heap. Once there, he was a foot beneath the ladder's break–off, even with arms stretched high and tight.

He was sure he could not negotiate a descent and reclimb without knocking down the pile.

He bent his knees, and tested the pile. It shuddered beneath him, but held. He tensed, bent at the knees again, and holding his breath, he leaped!

His fingertips touched the ragged edges of the ladder, and then slipped. The world dropped away. Kicking the pile of rubble into all corners of the plot room, he crashed to the deck. He lay there, silently, feeling the pain throb in his head and spine, and the voice that came down from above was mocking:

"Glad I don't have to depend on *you*, Corny."

The voice did not register. The voice was something he had managed to forget in the space of a few hours. But the word did it. That word Rennert had often used; knowing in its use he was hurting Cornfeld.

The astrogator looked up, the pains still flashing brightly behind his eyes, and saw the face, framed in the opening at the top of the downladder. Rennert was alive. Cornfeld gasped, his back hurt unmercifully.

"Just lie still, I'll be down in a second," Rennert grinned that wide, white infectious grin of superiority. He disappeared.

An instant later a pair of heavily–muscled legs in jump–shorts—bloody jump–shorts—appeared in the opening, and the magno–sole sneakers gripped at the top rungs of the downladder.

He descended quickly, to the end of the whole sections, and then dropped athletically, grasping at the last moment for the bottom rung. He hung suspended there, swaying slightly, then dropped the rest of the way to the deck, agilely avoiding Cornfeld and the bits of rubble beneath him. He landed with knees bent, and came erect with a leopard–like smoothness.

Rennert stood there and chuckled softly. "Honest to God! I mean honest to *God*, Corny!" as though he were the father of a mischievous boy. He bent to help Cornfeld to his feet.

Cornfeld felt a staggering loathing come over him. "Let me alone," he snapped out, ending the phrase with a raw gasp as his back throbbed painfully.

Rennert shrugged and backed away.

Cornfeld tried to get up. His back flamed incredibly, but he was sure he had broken nothing. As he struggled to rise, Rennert went about the plot room methodically, till he found what he was seeking, a deck of scratchbutts, in a still–closed drawer.

He drew one out with two fingers and scratched it alight on the magno–sole of his sneaker.

As he lifted his foot for the motion, Cornfeld saw the nasty gash that had been ripped in the man's left thigh. The blood was still pulsing warmly down Rennert's leg.

Rennert took a deep drag on the butt and offered it to Cornfeld. "Smoke?"

Cornfeld shook his head no, got one arm under himself, and heaved to his feet. He squealed sharply, and then it was all right. He was on his feet.

"I thought you were dead up there."

Rennert shook his head. "No such luck. The good, remember? They're the ones who get it young. Guys like me live to be a hund—"

Cornfeld cut him off. To hell with Rennert's wise remarks. "Iris is outside. Both her legs are broken, I think."

"Hey, where is she?" Rennert said, the concern reflected in his deep voice.

Cornfeld knew what was in Rennert's mind, knew it was playing its chess game, five moves ahead, and he knew he was losing again—if he had not *already* lost—as he always lost. He turned away, and limped toward the plot–bucket, slumping into it with a sigh, resting his back. "She's in the shade of a fin out there. I thought you were dead." He knew he was being repetitious, but what did it matter?

"I got wedged into the collar between sections," Rennert explained, hitching at his jump–shorts. "When the crash came I went out. I came to with a chunk of surfacing plate on my belly.

"I worked it off, and then fainted again. I guess I was just getting free when you started to pile those things up. Noble of you to think of me." He grinned wolfishly.

"Didn't you hope I'd been lost, Corny? Then you could have Iris all to yourself. Even with a pair of busted legs she's a pretty good lay."

"Shut up, will you, Rennert!" Cornfeld turned away, squirming in the chair. Partially because he could see the naked unpleasant-ness of Rennert's character, and partially because what Rennert said was true. He hated himself, at that moment, far more than he hated Rennert.

"Have it your way, Lancelot." And Rennert moved quickly through the rubble to the rent in the hull. He disappeared through it, into the heat of the alien day.

Cornfeld sat very still for some time, wondering.

Night had fallen more swiftly than he had thought possible, out on the dunes. And with the night came a humidity, stealing out of the rank jungle beyond. Deep in there, alien beasts struggled for suprema-cy, ripped, tore, killed and were, in turn, themselves killed. The stench of it, the sound of it, rose against the night sky, overpoweringly.

Iris Crosse lay against the cooling metal of the fin, her face drawn in the firm light of a lectrotorch stuck to the hull. Her legs had been tended with plastic splints from the first aid kit, and with the poultice Cornfeld had given Rennert to apply, there was no doubt her bones would knit properly in a few weeks.

But for now, her strength was drained, her blood ran slowly, there was a coolness about her.

Rennert crouched over a makeshift brazier from the ship's stores, cooking three strip steaks. Cornfeld was behind them, directly in the light of the torch, tinkering with the inverspace radio. Finally, as the scent of the jungle mingled alarmingly with the odors of the cooking steaks, he straightened and said, "I'm afraid we won't be stranded here after all. It works just fine. It was cushioned on its buffers, didn't even shake loose a circuit. All I have to do is call back to the relay station on Point George, let them know we're here, and they'll send out a beacon ship for us."

Iris raised her dark eyes to him, and the faint edge of a smile crossed her thin lips. Cornfeld felt ill at ease. "That's good," she said.

Rennert's masculine chuckle floated to them across the shadows, and he gave a massive halloo. "We're saved!" he clowned. "Saved from the ravages of the alien world!" His hand dipped toward the brazier, and when the fork came up, a deeply–charred strip steak dangled from the tines. "But right now . . . soup's on!"

Cornfeld was left to take his own as Rennert slapped steaks on disposable platters and moved next to the woman. Even though their relationship was one built on hatred and lust, Cornfeld knew he could be nothing to either of them. Not buffer, not catalyst, not deterrent, nothing. To them, he was there/not there.

Finally, because it seemed he must say *something*, so contained were they in theft little game of no–notice, Cornfeld ventured: "I'll call Point George."

Neither answered him. Iris Crosse looked up with a half–smile that said do what you wish if you wish, more of condescension than interest. Rennert did not bother to leave his food for a moment.

Finally, with effort, for they watched him without watching, Cornfeld rose, setting aside the platter, and said, "I'll call them now." He picked up the radio.

He walked around the rim of the ship, still and deep in the golden sand, and bent to enter the rip in the hull. Something moving at the far right edge of his vision brought him erect, hands on either side of the tear in the metal.

He turned his head quickly, and caught the flicker of it, at the edge of the jungle. What it was, he could not tell in the faint moonlight tattered by the feathery treetops. But it was there. Not heat dancers as he had thought earlier. Something was out there.

Was it danger? If it was, they would find out soon enough. He entered the ship.

He set the inverspace radio into its mounts. It was able to thrust its sorting beams through space (and not–space *between* space). He set it back between two buffer guards, cushioned on all sides. A set of eighteen verniers paraded across its face like an orderly progression of top–hatted men.

Bolted to the face of the machine were computed signals for all the major relay stations on the Rim. Cornfeld ran a stubby finger down the list, pausing at Point George to take the reading. He dialed it out and set the range and directional meters to full output. There was little hope of gauging how much matter–interference this planet contained in its soil composition, with the analyzers ruined. He set the inverad at full scope and drive, and clicked it on.

The response was immediate.

Almost immediately, a bounce signal returned and came out strong on the control room's beep system. It was the bounce signal for *standby*, indicating Point George was on the beam, and turning precedence calls over before accepting Cornfeld's.

Cornfeld dialed out a *crash red!* and the precedence signal for *standby* changed to *acceptance immediate*. A voice cut through the signal and rang loud in the control room:

"Point George acceptance. Go ahead. Point George acceptance. We read you, feature strong, signal clear, go ahead."

Cornfeld bent to the speak–tip and spoke in the tones he had been instructed to use over inverad. Calm, detached, authoritative: "This is Surveyship Charlie X–ray Delta niner fi–yive six six calling Point George. Do you read, Point George?"

The voice came back after a split–instant's time–lapse as the message sped through inverspace. "We read you, Charlie X–ray Delta niner five six six. Go ahead."

Cornfeld edged the bucket up closer to the console and passed across his word. "We are down in disabled condition on co–ordinates . . . " he paused a moment to consult the Celestial Atlas for approximate readings, checked the readings with what coursecomp dials were still intact, and fed the data across.

Point George was silent a long minute and then, just as Cornfeld began to wonder if the beam had died, they came back: "Point George to CXD 9566. We have you spotted on the boards. Take it easy, mister, got a beam–spitter comin' in on you. Figure a week, at the outside. Do you need anything? Medic? Innoc–beads? Just name it, fella."

"We're fine," Cornfeld assured the nameless voice. "Plenty of rations, and no injuries we haven't already ministered to. Do you need any pin–point directions?"

Point George made a ticking sound as though considering his question, and then asked, "You're the fifth world out from a type G, aren't you?"

Cornfeld considered the sun that burned down from the sky each day, and answered, "Right. Type G. I don't know if we're fifth out . . . we were all unconscious when we came in. Is that what your readings on my beam say?"

Point George: "Check."

Cornfeld: "Then that's us. We're on the shore of a pretty big body of water. Jungle beyond the sand. That might help a little."

"It helps a lot, fella. Anything else?"

Cornfeld: "No, that's it. You figure we'll be picked up inside a week?"

Point George: "That's what Clearance just reported. The spitbeam is bouncing now. They had a ship out near Kasca IV. Figure the normal invertime and a week or thereabouts ought to see you on the way back."

Cornfeld: "Thanks a lot, Point George." His voice was ripe with gratitude and undisguised relief, "This is CXD 9566 over and out."

The *cutaway* signal filled the room, and Cornfeld snapped the inverad off. He slumped back in the bucket. For some unreasonable reason, he had been at ease since he had found the inverspace radio intact, knowing they could get through; but only now, with the rescue beam–spitter bouncing out to them, was he untensed, secure again. *He realized, abruptly and with a shocking coldness, for the first time in his life, how terrified he was of reality and the confusion of situations in which he was a pawn. Insecure. Frightened. Not weak, but needing order and stability.*

Quiet, peace of mind, order, quiet.

The scream rang out in the night, building, climbing, spiralling till it was choked off by vocal cords that could stretch no tighter. Iris Crosse had seen horror.

The sound paralyzed him for a second, and then he was tripping over broken bits of ship accoutrements, stumbling to the opening in the hull and pausing there, hands frozen on either side of the rip, staring into the dunes.

What had been movement—what had been heat–lightning or dust shimmering—had now fully materialized, at last revealed itself, was now near enough to be labelled as what it really was.

Ants!

A horde of ants. A wave of ants. A sea, a torrent, a world of ants. A million and another million and a billion ants, tumbled crowded jammed one atop another. An army, drawn up just on the other side of the dune on which Iris Crosse propped against the ship's fin. They were moving and moving and moving, yet they were still. Each creature had individual movement, but the mass was still, not advancing.

Iris Crosse was white in the shadow of the ship's fin. There in the moonlight, her body twitching with uncontrolled horror, her hand fisted between her teeth, her eyes great dark inkblots above alabaster cheeks, the strong woman sat and struggled in the grip of a hundred thousand volts of terror.

"Iris!" Rennart screamed, "Get up! Get up!" He yelled, but he did not move from the two–foot area beyond the opening in the hull. Cornfeld realized, even as Rennert's hysterical shriek cut the night, that Iris *couldn't* move—two splinted legs stretched out before her. But neither did he make the move to rescue her. Both men stood staring at her.

Staring at the sea of ants—or something *like* ants—so near to her. So near to overflowing, to picking her young body clean of flesh and firmness. In his mind, Cornfeld could see the naked land after an attack of the army ants. His mind saw the eyeless sockets jabbed in the skull of what had once been Iris Crosse.

Yet he stood there, unmoving. Why was that?

Then, without any warning, as one, the ants moved.

They surged and churned and roiled and *moved*.

Back into the jungle.

Cornfeld realized someone was giggling hysterically, teeth chattering. The ants were almost entirely gone before he recognized the mad little titter as his own.

After Rennert had gone into the jungle and snatched up a dozen of the ant–like creatures, he brought them back in a specimen cradle, for Iris Crosse's examination.

Her stateroom was split in half. One compartment held living accommodations, and the section behind the accordion–door was a compact laboratory.

It was to this lab that Rennert and Cornfeld carried Iris, their arms locked hand–on–wrist to make a seat for her. The specimen cradle was brought in by Wayne Rennert and deposited beside the woman.

She sat on a high stool, her legs straight out before her, under the bench, awkwardly, as she prepared slides and gauging devices from the clipboards above the bench.

"I'd like to be alone, do you mind?" She did not bother to ask; it was merely an impolite directive. Rennert chuckled nastily and—accidentally?—his arm brushed a stand of test tubes as he went out. They crashed to the deckplate and bounced madly around the laboratory.

He was gone, and Cornfeld, feeling foolish, bent to pick them up. A vague, "Thank you," edged with ice–crystals, came from her, but she did not look up.

He left the laboratory quietly.

The ants returned the next day, and the next. On a short safari paralleling the edge of the sea for a mile, and then into the rim of the dessicated area at the edge of the jungle, Rennert and Cornfeld saw the great hordes many times.

Then, three days after Iris Crosse had begun her experiments on the ants, two things happened.

As they came down the side of a dune, they stopped abruptly, for the golden sands were dark with the ant horde. "Again?" Rennert snorted, and started to turn away.

Cornfeld continued walking. It was something—what?—that made him what could he call it? want to *know* these odd ant–like creatures. He could not put it into words, but there was a drawing from them, to him, and back to them again. He walked toward them slowly.

"What the hell is with you, Cornfeld? You want to get chewed up or something?" He continued to curse, trying to stop Cornfeld, but the shorter man was determined.

"Leave me alone, Rennert. Get away." Rennert tried to land a right cross on Cornfeld's jaw, but the shorter man stepped out of the path of the blow easily.

Then Cornfeld was near enough. A good thirty feet still separated him from the dark inkstain that covered the dunes from the edge of the sea to the rim of the jungle. But he was near enough.

What was between them . . . what began with the ants . . . and was magnified in him . . . and was returned to the ants . . . was strong enough. A feeling of infinite sadness welled over Cornfeld and

the weeping woman clothed in grey sheets came toward them, her face hung about with monstrous shadows, her features contorted with the sorrow that ate at her. There had been death and sadness unable to be borne. A dam had burst inside her, and the world had lost all light. Oh, God! The misery, the aching, the loneliness and the hunger for no–sorrow. The weeping woman clutched at her streaming hair, and pulled at her cadaverous grey bindings. She stopped, there before the two men — Cornfeld living in the sorrow he felt; Rennert a study in terror as this image came on — and her throat stretched tight as old leather, while her chin turned up to the sun, and her eyes exploded with tears and her mouth's gash was a black entry to nothing. The sorrow boiled and broiled in her, rising to a hysterical pitch, as Cornfeld

felt the sorrow pass, and the woman disappear. Gone!

Rennert's mouth was wide open. That was the first thing Cornfeld saw as the emotion of sadness drained out of him, leaving him vessel–empty, eyes burning. He dropped to his knees, stiffly, and remained there.

"You're crazy!" Rennert sobbed.

as

the madman gibbered across the sands at them. His rags gave off the smell of dung, and his hair was unkempt, flowing about him from head to shoulders, his hands wicked claws that rent the air as he screamed and laughed and cavorted toward them in a frenzy of maniacal destruction. Rennert screamed, and the thought of Cornfeld's insanity faded

to the accompaniment of

the fading of the crazed one. The sand was clean and silent once more, save the dark cancer of the ant horde, still there, still commanding.

"Devils!" Rennert shrieked and

the devils appeared, a horde of them, over a hundred, in the classical connotation of satanism. Red–skinned, horns jutting from foreheads, tails snapping with diamond–pointed barbs at the end . . .

Rennert made a strangled noise, and charged directly into them shrieking, "Hiyahh! Hiyahhh! Hi! Hi!" and began to stomp the ants. Under his boots the tiny creatures were crushed and beaten flat and dark blood drenched his boots. He jumped and leaped, ignoring the devils that milled about, uncertainty furrowing their crimson brows, their pitchforks clutched awkwardly, as though they should have been trumpets or rolling pins. Rennert shrieked insanely, drunk with the fury of hatred for the little creatures that did not move from beneath his crushing onslaught.

The devils disappeared and a great death's head was there, unmoving, with a quizzical expression on its fleshless face.

Cornfeld got to his feet, unstuck the ball peen hammer from his tool–belt, and calmly tracked down the slope of the dune to Rennert's mad thrashings. Hundreds of thousands of ant creatures had been stomped to greasy blackheads against the flesh of the dunes.

Cornfeld grasped the head of the hammer, and clubbed not too gently with the handle—behind Rennert's left ear.

The handsome man slumped forward, his face crushing a few more ants, as the death's head disappeared, and the ant horde moved out. The black shadow of them wallowed across the sand, and into the jungle, and was gone.

Cornfeld replaced the hammer, and stooped to grasp one of Rennert's arms. Carefully avoiding the dark goo that dripped from Rennert's boots, Cornfeld hoisted the pilot to his shoulders.

It was not a long walk to the ship. It only seemed that way.

She was cursing. Her mouth was a thin whip of crimson that flailed Rennert again and again, till her throat could contain no further moisture. Then she stopped and raised ineffectual fists to his ruggedly handsome face.

"Fool!" Vicious beyond compare. "Fool! We've come across something so unbelievable a million years of scientists would trade their souls and skills to see it . . . and *you!* you, you *vermin!* You kill them . . . kill them! Step on them as though they *were* ants. God knows how many of them you killed.

"Pray God it wasn't enough to damage the group mind. Because if you did, Wayne Rennert, you maniac! If you did! I'll see you're broken for it."

She subsided, and when it seemed she was finished, she whirled as far as her broken legs would allow, and commanded him, "Come here. Both of you. Just come over here and see this!"

Cornfeld came forward, was stopped by a flat hand against his chest as Rennert moved in front of him. "After me."

Rennert bent to the binocular eyepiece of the instrument.

Rennert looked up with annoyance. "So cut the damned melodrama; what am I supposed to see . . . besides a bug with a crewcut and a hundred eyes?"

"The crewcut—that isn't *hair!* They're sensitivity antennae."

"So?"

"Oh, God!"

"You mean it took you three days to figure out these damned things have antennae where they should have hair?"

"It took me three days to figure out that these bugs—well, they're not really bugs, either, but that's something else again—anyway, it took me three days to realize that each of these creatures is—"

Rennert burst in, snidely. "Sex–starved."

"—part of a group mind," she finished, her dark eyes smoldering with anger now. "Do you understand what I'm saying? Each bug is a segment of the greatest gestalt mind imaginable."

Cornfeld's gasp escaped despite his attempt to stifle it. "You're saying these bugs *think?*"

"That's just what I'm *not* saying. They can't think; they're idiot minds, separately. They have no more thought than the ants they resemble. But put them together, by the thousands, the millions, and they have a means of defense, a means of pseudo–communication."

Cornfeld was gripped with interest, ignoring with pointedness Rennert's snort of humor. "They can communicate? Speech, thought, what?"

She shook her head. "No, they don't have separate thoughts, or even one great group–thought. But put them together, and they become a great mental mirror, absorbing the thoughts and mind–images of any creatures within their range, and they reflect them back, make them almost substantial."

"That was the weeping woman, and the maniac, and the dev—" Cornfeld began. Rennert's snort of disgust cut him off.

"Prove it."

So she proved it. She took three of the ant–like creatures and put them together inside a tiny crystal sphere, under an amalgam of instruments that propagated a blue field of energy. The powers of the creatures were magnified, and after Cornfeld and Rennert had seen the slack–jowled hyena, the whispering wall of water, the three-winged dragonfly that divided into five, and the rubies that grew from air, they accepted what she had said.

That was the second thing that happened that day.

It had become a game.

Cornfeld and Rennert went out often, to test the gestalt reflectivity of the ant–colony mind. At first, as with any new encountering, the ants had not known how to get to the thoughts and mind–images of the Earthmen—which had been the reason they had not seen images the first time the ants came—but their drawing or "grab–power" as Iris called it, strengthened, and they dealt back the thoughts and visions of the two men with ease.

Iris Crosse's legs had nearly knitted. She was still confined to the ship, but she was able to move her legs without too much pain. It was this that caused her spirits to lift, and her manner of speech, which had been distinctly cool and antagonistic, to lighten. She would often not realize it when she called Rennert, "Wayne," or even "hon," and her lapsing into these familiarities—without a similar friendliness to Cornfeld—made him more withdrawn and brooding.

Iris could be heard laughing gaily in her laboratory, after Rennert had returned to her from a Visioning—as the trips had grown to be called—with detailed accounts of what he had done. It was during one of these sessions, late in the evening, that it happened.

Cornfeld was lounging half–in, half–out of the ship, his legs dangling a foot above the warm evening sands. He hardly noticed when Iris Crosse's resonant laughter tinkled hesitantly into awkward silence. But his mind resigned itself, and only subliminally did he hear her annoyed exclamation; another; her request in strained tones that Wayne *stop*. And then Cornfeld heard her scream.

It was that same nightmare, come to haunt him again.

He swung his legs up into the ship, and slammed through the tilting corridor toward the tiny laboratory.

Rennert had not even paid him the compliment of locking the stateroom. It stood open, and Iris Crosse was in plain sight, lying across her bunk, her chiton about her hips, her hair wild and dark, while she struggled with Rennert between her legs.

Cornfeld came through the doorway at a dead run and laid both hands with a thwack across the bigger man's shoulders. He heaved back, and Rennert's hands untangled themselves from the woman's clothing. He lost balance, and came tumbling back on Cornfeld. Cornfeld stepped to the side; the larger man fell to the deck.

He tried to rise, and Cornfeld brought up his booted foot, catching Rennert across the bridge of the nose. The captain of the ship squealed high and soprano, and fell back, clutching his broken nose. He lay there whimpering.

Iris Crosse sprawled across her bunk; she too whimpered.

Cornfeld stared at them. Both of them. God, how these two deserved each other.

Rennert could not be blamed entirely. She had no doubt flirted and goaded him, till he had lost his sense of right and propriety. But then, had he ever *really* had such a sense? Rennert was not of that cut. She lay there, her legs still splinted in the healing packs, and her white thighs were only cream against the whiter material of the splint–packs.

"You maniac!" Cornfeld found himself yelling at Rennert, lying at his feet. "You maniac! You couldn't wait. You had to try it now, didn't you? You had to have her again before the beamspitter got here, wasn't that it? You scum . . . she's in splints, you scum, in splints yet, can't you see?"

Fury drained through him. He dragged Rennert up by the collar, and forced his head toward the woman, lying disheveled, wracked by sobs, on her bunk.

Then Rennert got to his feet.

His face had crumbled and all expression but self–pity and degradation were gone. His nose was streaming crimson down across his tunic, and he made no effort to staunch the violent flow.

He stared at her an instant, and then, without his head turning, he stared at Cornfeld, livid in his wrath. Without warning, without preamble, he turned and ran from the lab–stateroom, the tool belt tinkling faintly at his waist.

Cornfeld heard his heavy boots go clattering down the decks, and then there was silence. He stared at the woman for an interminable, obstinately endless second, and then left the cabin.

He found Rennert far over the dunes, silvered like a fish thrown up on a beach, there in the moonlight, standing silent, staring off across the great ocean without a name. In that moment he felt a compassion, a nearness, a warmth and kinship, almost a brotherhood, with this big, amoral man.

He came up behind him, and was about to speak, when he realized abruptly that the ants were there, too. A great living body of them, stretching almost out of sight, from dune to dune, and from jungle's edge to nearly where the great waves hummed into silence on the beach.

He saw Rennert and he saw the ants, and what came to him came unbidden. "Ask *them*, Rennert. Go ahead. Ask *them* what you are. Ask them to show you what you are inside, the image of yourself. Ask them, Rennert."

The big man turned to Cornfeld, and his broken face was shining with blood in the moonlight. He turned slowly back again, and it was so apparent. He was thinking.

The tools on his belt glittered softly in the moonlight.

The ants were all darkness and life . . . and truth.

After it was over, Cornfeld returned to the ship. To wait. The beam-spitter had to come now. Fate had delayed it just long enough.

He came into Iris Crosse's stateroom, and she had pulled down her garments, and was lying with eyes closed on the bed. Drained of emotion, he no longer saw her as an object of desire. She was what she was, and he could not hate her.

But neither could he love her.

He wondered if he would love at all, for a great while.

She looked up, then, and her face had dark, dirty rivulets where tears had washed to their end, down her cheeks and into the corners of her mouth.

"Where is he?" she asked.

He did not answer, but turned to the lab table where a book had been turned over to maintain its place. He fingered the book absently.

"Where is he?"

After a pause, he answered, "He won't be coming back."

She stared at him with her wide, dark eyes that had once been beautiful, and could no longer understand. "What do you mean? Where is he?"

"He's dead."

Her mouth opened, and her hand had no place to find peace. It roved to her mouth, her eyes, her throat. Softly: *"You killed him!"*

Cornfeld was not aroused or surprised by her emotions, her tone, her attitude. It fit. It was natural. He shook his head somberly. "No."

"Then tell me, what happened, tell me!" she shrieked, her face the white of death and stillness.

"He killed himself. He used the Phillips head from his tool belt. He stabbed himself in the throat. It took him a long time to die, he—"

Her scream choked away his words. He had been speaking for himself, but her scream was the end of that too.

"Dead! OhmyGod, he killed himself, why, but why, oh God, *why?"*

Cornfeld started to leave.

The beamspitter would be here soon. He could stay in another section of the ship till it arrived, and not have to see her. It would make things easier. And then, when he got back to soil that was familiar, he would go and find some bar to drink in. Some dark bar, where no one knew him, and he could lose his identity thoroughly, for a good long while. But till then, he had to get away from her and the things she would know, that he would tell her.

Her voice stopped him in the doorway. "Why? Why did he do it? You *tell* me!" A little girl demanding to know who had broken her dolly.

He decided, before he went away from her, to kill that little girl; kill her completely. He turned back, and very calmly said:

"He killed himself because the ants showed him what he was. What he really was. As much truth as a man can stand and then some. They showed him the essence of himself."

The dawning of comprehension was not swift enough for him, and he spelled it out with brutal simplicity.

"The ants took his thoughts and his nature, and they fed them back to him as an image. Too much truth, Iris. Too much for a man like Rennert. He couldn't rationalize it when it got that bad; it was the full picture of how someone else saw him. *He killed himself because they showed him the image of the incarnation of evil."*

And the little girl died, as the man had died, because the realization was there that sometime, before the rescue ship came, she would have to know about herself; she would have to go out there and let the ants show her truth.

And Cornfeld silently prayed he would not do the same.

He went away from her, then; he went to lie down, hoping there was a future, but doubting it; really doubting it.

Now the book starts getting into the nitty-gritty. This is, I think, one of the best stories I've ever written. It is certainly one of the most personally important to me. It saved my sanity. It is a fantasy, of sorts, but a special kind, It is a terror of the mind. In several senses of the phrase. First, because it deals with the nightshade terrain within the thoughts. And second, because the thoughts were mine. This story grew out of a period of emotional stress after the breakup of my second marriage. I was legally separated, living alone in Los Angeles, finding it difficult to get work, and trying to run away from my own inability to cope by the senseless expedient of screwing every woman I could get my hands on. Then I began having a series of dreams; they continued for several months until, in mindless terror, I fled to the typewriter and wrote this story. When I completed it, the dreams were gone, never again to recur. There is much to be said for self-therapy. It may even be instrumental in helping someone nearing The Edge to get straight once more, to rid him of, say, a

LONELYACHE

The form of the habit she had become still drove him to one side of the bed. Despite his need for room to throw out arms, legs in a figure–4, crosswise angled body, he still slept on only one side of the big double bed. The force of memory of her body there, lying huddled on the inside, together cuddled body–into–body, a pair of question marks, whatever arrangement it might have been from night to night—still, her *there*. Now, only the memory of her warmth beside him kept him prisoner on his half. And reduced to memories and physical need for sleep, he retired to that slab of torture as seldom as possible. Staying awake till tiny hours, doing meaningless things, laughing at laughers, cleaning house for himself with methodical surgical tidiness till the pathology of it made him gibber and caper and shriek within his skull and soul, seeing movies that wandered aimlessly, hearing the vapors of night and time and existence passing by without purpose or validity. Until finally, crushed by the weight of hours and decaying bodily functions, desperately needing recharge, he collapsed into the bed that he loathed.

To sleep on one side only.

To dream his dreams of brutality and fear.

This was the dream, that same damned recurrent dream, never *quite* the same dream—but on the same subject, night after night, chapter after chapter of the same story: as if he had bought a book of horror stories; they would all be on one theme, but told differently; that was the way with this string of darkside visions.

Tonight came number fourteen. A clean–cut collegiate face proudly bearing its wide, amiable grin. A face topped by a sandy brush–cut and light, auburn eyebrows, giving that sophomoric countenance

94

a giggly, innocent vividness instantly conveying friendship. Under other circumstances Paul knew he could be close friends with this guy. *Guy*, that was the word he used, even in the dream, rather than *fellow*, or *man*, or—most accurately—*assassin*. In any other place than this misty nightmare, with any other intent than this one, they might have lightly punched each other's biceps in camaraderie and hey, how the hell are you'd each other. But this was the dream, latest installment, and this college guy was number fourteen. Latest in an endless, competent string of pleasant types sent to kill Paul.

The plot of the dreams was long–since formulated, now merely suggested by rote in the words and deeds of the players (sections indefinite, details muzzy, transitions blurred, logic distorted dream–style): Paul had been a member of this gang, or group, or bunch of guys, whatever. Now they were after him. They were intent on killing him. If they ever came at him in a group, they would succeed. But for some reason that made sense only in the dream, they were assigned the job one by one. And as each sweet human being tried to tip him the black spot, Paul killed him. One after another, by the most detailed, violently brutal and gut–wrenching means available, he killed the killers. Thirteen times they had come against him—these men who were decent and pleasant and dedicated, whom he would have been proud to call his friends under other circumstances—and thirteen times he had escaped assassination.

Two or three or—once—four in a night, for the past several weeks (and that he had only killed thirteen till now bore witness to the frequency with which he avoided sleep entirely, or crashslept himself into exhaustion so there *were* no dreams).

Yet the most disturbing part of the dreams was the brutalized combat itself. Never a simple shooting or positive poisoning. Never an image that could be re–told when awakening without bringing a look of shock and horror to the face of Paul's confidante. Always a bizarre and minutely–described *affaire de morte*.

One of the assassins had pulled a thin, desperately–sharp stiletto, and Paul had grappled with the man interminably, slashing at his flesh and the sensitive folds of skin between fingers, till the very essence, the very *reality* of death by knife became a gagging tremor in his sleeping body. It was as though the sense, the *feel* of death–in–progress was evoked. More than a dream, it had been a new threshold of anguish, a vital new terror which he would ever after have to support. It was something new to live with. Until finally he had locked the man's hands about the hilt and driven the slim blade into his stomach, deep and with difficulty, feeling it puncture and gash through organs and resisting, rubbery organs. Then pulling it away from the mortally–wounded assassin and (did he, or did he suppose he had) used it again and again, till the other had fallen under the furniture. Another had been battered to his knees and dispatched finally, with a smooth, heavy piece of black statuary. Still another had gone screaming, pushed abruptly (Paul with teeth bared, fang–like, vicious animal) from a ledge, twisting and plunging heavily away. The passion with which he had watched that body fall, the desire in him to *feel* the weight of it going down, had been the disgusting detail of that particular segment. Still another had come at Paul with some now–forgotten weapon, and Paul had used a tire chain on him, first wrapping it tightly about the assassin's neck and twisting till the links broke skin . . . then flaying the unconscious body till there was no life left in it.

One after another. Thirteen of them, two already tonight, and now number fourteen, this pleasant–enough guy with the rah–rah demeanor, and the fireplace poker in his competent hands. The gang would never let him alone. He had run, had hidden, had tried to avoid killing them by putting himself out of reach, but they always found him. He went at the guy, wrested the poker from him, and jabbed sharply with the pike–tip of it. He was about to envision where he had thrust that blunt–sharp point, when the phone went off and the doorbell rang— simultaneously.

For a screaming instant of absolute terror he lay there flat on his back, the other side of the bed creased only by a small furrow made by his spastic arm as it had flung itself away from him; the other side of the bed that she had inhabited, now untenanted, save for the wispy end–tips of the dream, streaking away as his arm had done.

While the chime and the bell rang in discordant duo.

Having saved him from seeing what damage he had done the collegiate guy's face. Almost like melodious saviors. Rung in by a watchful God who allotted only certain amounts of fear and depravity to each sleeptime. Knowing he would pick up the thread of the dream precisely where he had left off, next time out. Hoping he could stave off sleep for a year, two years, so he would not have to find out how the rah–rah type had died. But knowing he would. Listening to the phone and the door-bell clanging at him. Having let them serve their purposes of wakening him, now fearing to answer them.

He flipped onto his stomach and reached out a hand in the darkness that did not deter him. He grabbed the receiver off its rest and yowled, "Hold it a minute, please," and in one movement flipped aside the clammy sheet, hit the floor and surely fumbled his way to the door. He opened it as the chime went off again, and in the light from the hall-way saw only a shape, no person. He heard a voice, made no sense of it, and said impatiently, "C'min, c'min already for Chri'sake an' shut the door." He turned away and went back to the bed, picked up the receiver he had tossed onto the pillow, and cleared phlegm from his throat as he asked, "Yeah, okay now, who's this?"

"Paul. Has Claire gotten there, is she there yet?" He felt bits of rock–salt in the corners of his eyes, and fingered them tighter into the folds of flesh as he tried to place the voice. It was someone he knew, a friend, someone —

"Harry? That's you, Harry?"

On the other end of the line, way out there in the night somehow, Harry Dockstader swore lightly, quickly. "Yeah, me, me already. Paul, is Claire there?"

Paul Reed was suddenly assaulted by the overhead light going on, and he snapped his eyes shut against the blaze, opened them, closed them again, and then finally popped them open completely to see Claire Dockstader standing at the switch by the front door.

"Yeah, Harry, she's here," then the weirdness of her being here came to him fully, and he demanded, "Harry, what the hell is going on, Claire's over here, why isn't she with you? Why's she here?"

It was an inane conversation, totally devoid of sense, but his syn-apses were not yet in focus. "Harry?" he repeated.

The voice on the other end snarled, gutturally.

Then Claire was coming across the room at him, wrathful and impatient, ferocious in demanding, *"Give me that phone!"* Each word sharply enunciated, much too fine for this hour of the morning, each syllable clear and harsh and very thin–lipped, only a woman's way. "Give me that phone, Paul. Let *me* talk to him . . . hello, Harry? You sonofabitch, go straight to fucking hell, die you bastard! Ooo, you *bas*–tard!"

And she literally flung the receiver onto the rest.

Paul sat on the edge of the bed, feeling himself naked from the waist up, feeling the rug under his bare feet, feeling that *no* woman should use language like that at this hour. "Claire . . . *what* the hell is going *on?*"

She stood trembling for a moment, valkyric in her fury, then stalked, half–stumbled, fell across the room into the easy chair. Upon touching the seat she burst into tears. "Ooo, the *bas*–tard," she repeated, not to Paul, not to the silent phone, to the air perhaps. "That lousy chaser, that skunk and his chippies, those *bums* he brings up to the house, Oh God Why'd I Ever Marry That Skunk!"

It was, of course, all laid out for Paul in that sentence, even without the particulars, even at that hour, and the ring of his own recent past was so clear he winced. The word *chaser* did it. His own sister had called him that when she'd heard he and Georgette were divorcing. That damned word: *chaser*. He could still hear it. It had hurt.

Paul rose from bed. The one–and–a–half in which he managed to live (now) alone suddenly seemed close and muggy with a woman in it. "Claire, want some coffee?"

She nodded, still running through her thoughts like prayer beads, eyes turned inward. He moved past her into the tiny kitchenette. The electric coffeepot was on the sideboard, and he hefted it, shoot it to see if there was enough left from the last brewing. A heavy sloshing reassured him, and he plugged in the cord.

As he returned to the living room, her eyes followed him. He dropped onto the bed and slid upward, bracing the pillow behind him. "Okay," Paul said, reaching for the cigarettes beside the phone, "lay it on me. Who was it this time, and how far along were they when you caught him?"

Claire Dockstader pursed her lips so tightly, dimples appeared in her cheeks. "Only a philanderer like you, as bad as Harry, just as big a Skunk, could put it that way!"

Paul shrugged. He was a long, lean man with a thatch of straw–colored hair; he raked the hair off his forehead and applied himself to lighting the cigarette. He didn't want to look at her. A thing in his living room, soon after Georgette, too soon, even a friend's wife. He pulled at the cigarette, and at his thoughts: neither satisfied. He seemed too long for the bed, ungainly, hardly of interest to a woman, yet apparently it was not so, for she stared at him differently now. A subtle shifting of mood in the room, as though she had suddenly realized she had not only broken into his living room, but into his bedroom as well, a room in which other things than just living were done. They were very close, but held apart by a circumstance that both realized might at any moment melt. Uncomfortable, suddenly, both of them. He pulled up the sheet to his waist; she looked away.

Coffee perking, popping, distracting, thank God.

"Christ, what time is it?" Paul asked (himself, in self–defense, more than her). He pulled the travalarm from the nightstand and stared into its face, its idiot face, as though the numbers meant something. "Jeezus, Jeezus, three ayem, Jeezus; don't you people ever sleep?" He was a pot, calling a kettle black. He never slept, never really went to bed, so who was he fooling with this line out of suburban rote?

She shifted in the easy chair, rearranging her skirt that had ridden up over her knees, and Paul once more marveled at the joys of the current hemlines, if one was a leg man, which he had decided with the advent of the current hemlines, he was. She caught his stare and toyed with it for a moment, then allowed it to vaporize in her own eyes, not just yet returning his proposition.

It was happening, just this easily. A pact of guilt and opportunity was being solidified, without the decency of either admitting its necessity. Paul had been separated not nearly long enough to attempt morality of a high order, and Claire was still burning with outrage. Neither would say the name of the game, but both would play, and both knew it would happen.

And as soon as Paul Reed admitted his loneliness, his guilt and his desires were compounding to produce (why fool around, name it!) adultery, an act of love performed without the catalyst of love, something unpleasant began to happen in the empty, dark, far corner of the room.

He was unaware of its beginnings.

"Why did you pick me for your flight?" he asked flippantly.

"You were the only one I could think of who'd be awake this late . . . and I wasn't thinking too clearly . . . I was too furious to think straight." She stopped talking; she had said much more than what she had said. Of all the places she might have gone, of all the seedy bars where she might have been picked up and laid in retaliation, of all the married friends she and Harry had accrued, of all the cheap hotels where an innocent night of sleep might be purchased for five dollars, she had picked Paul and his living room that was a bedroom that was a hole in the world where guilt could be born out of frustration and pain.

"Is that, uh, coffee ready?" she asked.

He slid out of bed, nakedly aware of her eyes on his body, and went into the kitchenette. He ached in places he did not want to ache, and knew what was going to happen, for all the wrong reasons, and knew he would despise not only her and himself when it had been done, when they had killed something between them, but that he would barely think of it again. He was wrong.

When he handed her the coffee cup, their hands touched, and their eyes locked for the first time in this new way, and the cyclic movement began for the millionth time that night. And once begun, the cycle could not be impeded.

While slowly, steadily, in the dark corner, what had begun to happen, nasty as it was, went unnoticed. Their insensate passion a midwife at that strange birth.

Simply the mechanics of divorce were gristmill enough to powder him into the finest ash. Simply the little pains of walking through the apartment where they had bumped into one another constantly, the lawyer talks, the serving of the papers, the phone calls that lacked any slightest tinge of communication, the recriminations, and worst of all, the steadily deteriorating knowledge that somehow what had gone wrong was not real, but a matter of thoughts, attitudes, dreams, ghosts, vapors. All insubstantial, but so omnipresent, so *real*, they had broken up his marriage with Georgette. As if they *were* substantial, rock–hard, real, physically tearing her from his arms and his thoughts and his life. Phantom raiders from both of their minds, whose sole purpose in life was to shrivel and shred and shatter their union. But the thoughts and vapors and grey images persisted, and he existed alone in the one–and–a–half where they had set up their gestalt, while she cast the runes and murmured the incantations and boiled up the mystic brews, all set down so precisely in the grimoire of divorce. And as the pattern of separation progressed, a boulder racing mindlessly downhill, needing only the most impossible strength imaginable to halt its crushing rush, his life set itself up in a new sequence, apart from her, yet totally motivated by her existence, and the reality of her absence.

Earlier that day he had received a phone call from her. One of those backbiting, bitter, flame–colored conversations that ended in him telling her to go to hell, she wasn't getting any more money out of him till the settlement, and he didn't give a damn *how* badly she needed it.

"The Court said sixty–five a month separate maintenance, and that's all you're getting. Stop buying clothes and you'll have enough to live on."

Chittering reply from the other end.

"Sixty–five baby, that's *it!* You're the one who moved out, not me; don't expect me to support your nutty behavior gratis. We're through, Georgette, get that through your platinum head, we're all done. I've had it with you! I'm fed up with all the dirty dishes in the sink, and your subway phobia, and not being able to touch your goddam hair after you've been to the beauty parlor and—oh, crap, why bother with all this . . . the answer is . . . "

Chittering interruption, vitriol electrically transmitted, hatred telephonically magnified, poured directly into his mind through his ear.

" . . . *yeah?* Well, the same to you, you stupid simple–ass broad, the same *double* to you. Go to hell! You're not getting any more money out of me till the settlement, and I don't give a damn *how* badly you need it!"

He had slammed the receiver back on the stand, and continued getting dressed for his date. When he had picked up the girl, a brunette he had met in his insurance agent's office, a secretary there, it was as though he was collecting unemployment, getting something to which he was entitled, but that nonetheless smacked faintly of being on relief.

Picking up this girl for the first time was precisely like collecting unemployment. Enough to keep him going, but not nearly enough to sustain him in a supportable life. A dole. A pittance, but desperately necessary. A casual girl, with a life of her own, whose path would cross his this once, and then they would stumble past, down their own roads forever, light–footed, unlighted, interminably.

"I'm afraid I won't be very charming company tonight," he told her as she slid into the car. "A woman who looks very much like you gave me considerable heartache today."

101

"Oh?" she inquired guardedly. It was their first date. "Who would that be?"

"My ex–wife," he said, telling her the first lie. He had not looked at her, save when he reached across to open the door. Now he stared dead–straight ahead as he pulled the unpolished Ford away from the curb and swung it into traffic.

She sat looking at him speculatively, wondering if accepting a dinner date with an office client was such a good idea after all, no matter *how* engaging a sense of humor he had. His face was not at all the youthful cleverness he had presented to her on those three occasions when he had come to the insurance office. It was a harder substance, somehow, as though whatever light, frothy matter had been its basic component previously, had congealed, like week–old gravy. He was unhappy and disturbed, of course, there was that in abundance; but something else skittered on the edge of his expression, a somnolence, and she was strangely frightened by it—though she was certain it meant harm not for her, but on the contrary, very much for him.

"Why do you let her give you heartache?" she asked.

"Because I still love her, I suppose," he answered, a bit too quickly, as though he had rehearsed it.

"Does *she* love you?"

"Yeah, I guess she does." He paused, then added in a contemplative monotone, "Yeah. I'm quite certain she does. Otherwise we wouldn't try to kill each other so hard. It's making us both very sick, her loving me."

She straightened her skirt and tried to find another passage through the conversation, but all she could think was, *I should have told him I was busy tonight.*

"Do I look very much like her?"

He stared straight ahead, handling the wheel casually, as though very certain, very sure of it, as though he derived a deep inner satisfaction from driving, from propelling all this weight and metal precisely as he wished. It was as though he was with her, yet very far away, locked in an embrace with his vehicle.

"Oh, not really, I suppose. She's blonde, you're brunette. Just around the temples, maybe, and your hair, the way you wear it pulled back on the side that way, and the skin around your eyes crinkled the same way. That, and the tone of your skin. Something like that; more *reminds* me of her than any actual look–alike."

"Is that why you asked me out?"

He thought about it a moment, pressing his full lips together, then replied, "No. That wasn't it. In fact, when I realized that you reminded me of her, I wanted to call the office and break the date." *I wish you had,* she thought severely, *I wish I weren't here. With you.*

"We don't have to go, you know."

He turned his head, then, seemingly startled. "What? Oh, say, *hell* I didn't mean to depress you. This thing has been going on for months, and it's just one of those miserable problems that has to work itself out. Don't think I was trying to wriggle out of buying you a meal."

"I didn't think *that,*" she replied coolly. "I merely thought you might want to be alone this evening."

He smiled, a strained little smile that was half frown and part sneer, and moved his head slightly. "Christ! Anything but *that.* Not alone. Not tonight."

She settled back against the vinyl seat cover, determined suddenly to make him uncomfortable, in defense.

What seemed to each of them like elastic hours stretched past, and then he said, in an altogether new tone of voice, a forced light tone each knew was false, "Where would you like to go? Chinese? Italian? I know a nice little Armenian restaurant . . . ?"

She was silent, purposefully, and it *served* its purpose; he was uncomfortable, unhappier than before, and in the next instant it passed and he felt hateful, outright nasty, wanting to either get her into bed at once, or dump her, but not have to suffer this way through an entire evening. And so she defeated herself, as the rock wall slid up to cover the gentleness he would have demonstrated later that night. Deviousness replaced gentleness, sadness.

"Listen," he said smoothly (once again, a new tone, a lacquer–finished tone, chromed and slick), lightly, "I didn't get a chance to shave before I picked you up, and I feel like a slob. You mind if we stop off for a minute at my place, and I'll run a razor over my face?"

She was not fooled. She had been married once, had been divorced, had been dating since she was fifteen, she knew *exactly* what he was saying. He was offering a private demonstration of his etchings. Her mind turned the offer slowly, examining it—in that breathless eternity of a moment in which all decisions are made—and studying each shimmering facet. She knew it was a bad idea, had no merit in any way, that she was a fool to think seriously of it, and that he would back off if she made the slightest sound of disapproval. True true, a bad idea, one to reject on the spot, and she rejected it. "All right," she said. He turned sharply at the next corner.

He looked down at her face, and abruptly saw her at the age of sixty–five. He knew with a crystal certainty what she would look like when she was old. Superimposed over the pale–and–pink firm immediacy of her face framed against the pillow, he saw a grey line–mask of the old woman she would one day become. The mouth with its stitchlines, tiny pickets running down into the lips; the dusty hollows lurking beneath the eyes; dark spaces in the character lines and in the planes of expression—as though whole sections had been sold off to retain life, even at the cost of losing appearance. The sooty patina covering the flesh, much like that left when a moth has been crushed, the powdery fine ash of its wings imprinting the surface on which the death had occurred. He stared down at her, seeing the double–image, the future lying inchoate across her now–face, turning the paramour beneath him into a relic of incognito spare parts and empty passions. A dim, drenched cobweb of probability, there in the eye–sockets, across the mouth he had kissed, radiating out from the nostrils and pulsing ever so faintly in the hollow of her throat.

Then the vision melted off her young face, and he was looking at the creature of empty purposes he had just used. There was a mad, insane light flickering out of her eyes. "Tell me you love me, even if you don't mean it," she murmured huskily.

There was a hungry urgency, a breathless demand in her voice, and a fist closed around his heart as she spoke, a chill ruined his aplomb, his grasp of the present, so recently returned to him. He wanted to pull out of her, away from her, as far as he could, and crouch down somewhere in the bedroom in a patient, foetal security.

But the corner of the room he might have chosen was already occupied. Darkly occupied by bulk and a sinister presence. The breathing in that corner was coming laboredly, but much more regularly than before; it seemed to have become more steady, pulsing, as they had entered the apartment; and during the parry and counter and riposte of their encounter it had metronomically hurried itself to a level of even oftenness. Oh, it was taking form, form, form.

Paul sensed it, but discounted the instinct.

Deep breathing, stentorian, labored—but becoming more regular. "Tell me. Tell me you love me, nineteen times, very fast."

"I love you I love you I love you I love you," he began rattling them off, propped on one elbow, counting them on the fingers of his left hand. "I love you I love you I luh—"

"Why are you counting them?" she demanded, coquettishly, in a bizarre grotesque parody of naiveté.

"I don't want to lose track," he answered, brutally. Then he slipped sidewise, falling onto his back, on Georgette's side of the bed (feeling uncomfortable there, as though the ridges and whorls of her body were imprinted there, making it lumpy for him, but with the determination not to let *this* girl lie on *that* side). "Go to sleep," he instructed her.

"I don't want to go to sleep."

"Then go bang your goddam head against the wall," he snapped. Then he was forcing himself to sleep. Eyes closed, knowing how angry the girl beside him had become, he commanded sleep to come, and timorously, fawn–like in a deep foreboding forest, it came, and touched him. So that he began to dream again. *That* dream, again.

In the eye, the right eye. The point of the poker entered, did its damage, came away foul. Paul flung himself violently from the sight, even as the crew–cut young man toppled suddenly past him, still alive somehow, crawling, dying by every bit of flesh through every rotting second. Starlight and darkness slipped by overhead as Paul whirled, spun, found himself in another place. A plaza, perhaps . . .

A crowd, down the smart sleek shop–bordered street—a posh street (where?) in Beverly Hills, perhaps, glistening and elegant, and seeming almost dazzlingly clean with rhodium–finished permanence—growling, coming toward him.

They were masked, caricatured, made up for some weird mardi gras, or costume party, or gathering of witches, where real faces would reveal real persons, and thus provide a grasp for their damnation. Strangers, boiling hurling sweeping down the street toward him in a chiaroscuro montage of chimerical madness. A vision out of Bosch; a bit of underdone potato or undigested Dali, hurled forth from a dream–image by Hogarth; a pantomime out of the innermost circle of Dante's Inferno. Coming for him. For him.

At last, after all these weeks, the dream had broken its pattern, and the massed terrors were now coming for him in a body. No longer one at a time, man–for–man in that never–ending succession of pleasant assassins. Now they had gathered together, grotesque creatures, masked and hungry.

If I can figure out what this means, I'll know, he thought suddenly. In the midst of the multi–colored haze of the dream, he knew abruptly, certainly, that if he could just make some sense from the events unreeling behind his eyes (and he *knew* it was a dream, right then), there would be a key to his problems, a solution that would work for him. So he concentrated. *If I can just understand who they are, what they're doing here, what they want from me, why they won't let me escape, why they're chasing me, what it takes to placate them, to get away from them, who I am who I am who I am . . . then I'll be free, I'll be whole again, this will be over, this will end, it'll end . . .*

He ran down the street, the white clean street, and dodged in and among the cars that had suddenly appeared in lines, waiting for the light to change. He ran down the street to the intersection, and cut across among the slowly–moving vehicles, terror clogging his throat, his legs aching from the running, seeking an escape, an exit, *any* exit—a place of rest, of security where he could close the door and know they could not get in.

"Here! We'll help you," a man shouted from a car, where he was packed in with his family, many children. Paul ran to the car, and the man opened his door, and Paul managed to crowd past him as he pulled the seat back, offering entrance to the back seat. Paul squeezed through, pushing the man up against the steering wheel. Then the seat was dropped back, Paul was in the rear with the children, and the car was piled with (what? fuzzy, indistinct) clothes, or soft possessions that the children sat on, and he was forced to lie down across the back deck, under the rear window

(but how could that be?

(he was a full–grown man, he couldn't squeeze himself into that small a space, the way he had when he had been a child and gone on trips with his mother and father and laid down under the back window because the back seat was filled up, the way it had been when his father had died, and he had gone away with his mother from their home to the new home . . .

(why did that memory suddenly come through so lucidly?

(was he a grown man, or a small child?

(*please* answer!) and he could see out the back window, and the crowd of terrifying masked figures, bright-eyed and haunting, were being left behind. Still, somehow, he did not feel safe! He was with the ones who could help, that man driving, he was strong and would drive fast through the traffic, and save Paul from the haunters, but why didn't he feel safe . . . why?

He woke, crying. The girl was gone.

There was one who chewed gum while they did it. An adolescent with oily thighs who had no idea of how to live in her body. The act was sodden and slow and entirely derelict in its duties. Afterward, he thought of her as a figment of his imagination, leaving only her laugh behind.

She had a laugh that sounded like pea pods snapping open. He had met her at a party, and her attractiveness stemmed chiefly from too many vodkas and tonics.

Another one was completely lovely, and yet, she was the sort of woman who gave the impression, upon entering a room, of having just left it.

One was small and slight and shrieked for no reason save that she had read how passionate women screamed at the climax—in a bad book. Or more aptly, an undistinguished book, for she was an undistinguished woman.

One after another they came to that one-and-a-half, casual adulteries without purpose or direction, and he indulged himself, again and again, finally realizing (by what was taking shape in the corner) what he was doing to himself, and his life that was no longer a life.

Genesis refers to sin that coucheth at the door, or croucheth at the door, and so this was no new thing, but old, so very old, as old as the senseless acts that had given it birth, and the madness that was causing it to mature, and the guilty sorrow—the lonelyache—that would inevitably cause it to devour itself and all within its sight.

On the night that he actually paid for love, the night he physically reached into his wallet and took out two ten dollar bills and gave them to the girl, the creature took full and final shape.

This girl: when "good girls" talk about "tramps" they mean this girl and her sisters. But there are no such things as "tramps" and even the criminal never thinks of himself in those terms. Working–girl, entrepreneur, renderer of services, smarty, someone just getting along . . . these are the ways of her thoughts. She has a family, and she has a past, and she has a face, as well as a place of sex.

But commercialism is the last sinkhole of love, and when it is reached, by paths of desperation and paths of cruel, misused emotions—all hope is gone. There is no return save by miracles, and there are no more miracles for the common among common men.

As he handed her the money, wondering why in God's name, *why!* the beast in the corner by the linen closet took its final shape, and substantiality, reality was its future. It had been called up by a series of contemporary incantations, conjured by the sounds of passion and the stink of despair. The girl snapped her bra, covered herself with dacron and decorum, and left Paul sitting stunned, inarticulate with terror in the presence of his new roommate.

It stared at him, and though he tried to avert his eyes (screams were useless), he stared back.

"Georgette," he said huskily into the mouthpiece, "listen . . . lis, *listen* to me, willya, for Christ's sake . . . st, stop *blab*bering for a second, willya, just, just SHUT UP FOR ONE GODDAM SECOND! will ya . . . " she finally subsided, and his words, no longer forced to slip themselves piecemeal between hers, left standing naked and alone with nothing but silence confronting them, ducked back within him, shy and trembly.

"Well, go *on,*" he said, reflexively.

She said she had nothing further to say; what was he calling her for, she had to get ready to go out.

"Georgette, I've got, well, I've got this uh this problem, and I had to *talk* to someone, you were the one I figured would understand, y'see, I've uh—"

She said she didn't know an abortionist, and if he had knocked up one of his bummy–girls, he could use a goddam coat–hanger, a *rusty* coat–hanger, for all she cared.

"No! No, you stupid ass, that isn't anything like what I'm scared about. *That* isn't it, and who the hell do *you* care who I date, you tramp . . . you're out on the turf enough for *both* of us . . . " and he stopped. This was how all their arguments had started. From subject to subject, like mountain goats from rock to rock, forgetting the original discussion, veering off to rip and tear with their teeth at each other's trivialities.

"Georgette, *please!* Listen to me. There's a, there's a thing, some kind of *thing* living here in the apartment."

She thought he was crazy, what did he mean?

"I don't know. I don't know what it is."

Was it like a spider, or a cat, or what?

"It's like a bear, Georgette, only it's something else, I don't know what. It doesn't say anything, just *stares* at me—"

What was he, cracking up or something? Bears don't talk, except the ones on TV, and what was he, trying to pull off a nut stunt so he wouldn't have to pony up the payments the court set? And why was he calling her in the first place, closing with: I think you're flipping, Paul. I always said you were a whack, and now you're proving it.

Then the phone clicked, and he was alone.

Together.

He looked at it from the corner of his eye as he lit a cigarette. Hunkered down in the far corner of the room, near the linen closet, the huge soft–brown furry thing that had come to watch him, sat silently, paws folded across its massive chest. Like some great Kodiak bear, yet totally unlike it in shape, the truncated triangle of its bloated form could not be avoided—by glance or thought. The wild, mad golden discs of its eyes never turned, never flickered, while it watched him.

(This description. Forget it. The creature was nothing like that. Not a thing like that at all.)

And he could sense the reproach, even when he had locked himself in the bathroom. He sat on the edge of the tub and ran the hot water till steam had obscured the cabinet mirror over the sink and he could no longer see his own face, the insane light in his eyes so familiar, so similar to the blind stares of the creature in the other room. His thoughts flowed, ran, lava–like, then congealed.

At which point he realized he had never seen the faces of any of the women who had been in the apartment. Not one of them. Faceless, all of them. Not even Georgette's face came to him. None of them. They were all without expression or recall. He had been to seed with so many angular corpses. The sickness welled up in him, and he knew he had to get out of there, out of the apartment, away from the creature in the corner.

He bolted from the bathroom, gained the front door without breaking stride, caroming off the walls, and was lying back against the closed slab of hardwood, dragging in painful gouts of air before he realized that he could not get away that easily. It would be waiting for him when he got back, whenever he got back.

But he went. There was a bar where they played nothing but Sinatra records, and he absorbed as much maudlin sorrow and self–pity as he could, finally tumbling from the place when the strings and the voice oozed forth:

How I wish I could forget
Those happy yesteryears,
That have left
A rosary of tears.

There was another place, a beach perhaps, where he stood on the sand, silent within himself, as the gulls wheeled and gibbered across the black sky, kree kree kree, driving him a little more mad, and he dug his naked hands into the sand, hurling great clots of the grainy darkness over his head, trying to kill those rotten, screaming harridans!

And another place, where there were lights that said things, all manner of unintelligible things, neon things, dirty remarks, and he could not read any of them. (In one place he was certain he saw the masked revelers from his dream, and frothing, he fled, quickly.)

When he returned, finally, to the apartment, the girl with him swore she wasn't a telescope, but yeah, sure, she'd look at what he had to show her, and she'd tell him what it was. So, trusting her, because she'd said it, he turned the key in the door, and opened it. He reached around the jamb and turned on the light. Yeah, yeah, there he was, there he was, that thing there he was, all right. Uh–huh, there he is, the thing with the staring eyes, there he is.

"Well?" he asked her, almost proudly, pointing.

"Well what?" she replied.

"Well what about *him?*"

"Who?"

"*Him*, him, you stupid bitch! Him right *there*! HIM!"

"Y'know, I think you're outta your mind, Sid."

110

"M'name's not Sid, and don't tell me you don't see him, you lying sonofabitch!"

"Say lissen, you *said* you was Sid, and Sid you're gonna be, and I don't see *no* goddam nobody there, and if you wanna get laid allright, and if you don't, just say so and we'll have another drink an' that'll be *that!*"

He screamed at her, clawing at her face, thrusting her out the door. "Get out, get outta here, g'wan, get out!" And she was gone, and he was alone again with the creature, who was unperturbed by it all, who sat implacably, softly, waiting for the last tick of time to detach itself and fly free from the fabric of sanity.

They trembled there together in a nervous symbiosis, each deriving something from the other. He was covered with a thin film of horror and despair, a terrible lonelyache that twisted like smoke, thick and black within him. The creature giving love, and he reaping heartache, loneliness.

He was alone in that room, the two of them: himself and that soft-brown, staring menace, the manifestation of his misery.

And he knew, suddenly, what the dream meant. He knew, and kept it to himself, for the meaning of dreams is for the men who dream them, never to be shared, never to be known. He knew who the men in the dreams were, and he knew now why none of them had ever simply been killed by a gun. He knew, diving into the clothes closet, finding the duffle bag full of old Army clothes, finding the chunk of steel that lay at the bottom of that bag. He knew who he was, he knew, he knew, gloriously, jubilantly, and he knew it all, who the creature was, and who Georgette was, and the faces of all the women in the damned world, and all the men in the damned dreams, and he had it all, right there, right in his hands, ready to be understood.

He went into the bathroom. He was *not* going to let that bastard in the corner see him succeed. He was going to savor it himself. In the mirror he now saw himself again. He saw the face and it was a good face and a very composed face, and he stared back at himself smiling, saying very softly, "Why did you have to go away?"

Then he raised the chunk of steel.

"Nobody, absolutely nobody," he said, holding the huge .45 up to his face, "has the guts to shoot himself through the eye."

He laid the hollow bore of the great blocky weapon against his closed eyelid and continued speaking, still softly. "Through the head, yeah sure, anybody. Or the guys with balls can point it up through the mouth. But through the eye, nobody, but *no*body." Then he pulled the trigger just as they had taught him in the Army; smoothly, evenly, in one movement.

From the other room came the murmur of breathing, heavily, stertorously, evenly.

Ted Sturgeon has said some strange things about this story in the Introduction to this book. He has said it is hallucinogenic in tone. He may be right, I don't know. I wrote it as a straight attempt at mysticism. But the style was experimental, as well. I employed a Baroque, even rococo approach. I wanted a density of images, a veritable darkness of language, comparable in narrative to what saxophonist John Coltrane blows in his "sheets of sound" style. That is, a laying on thickly of impressions, one atop another, like the scales of an armadillo. It was published in Knight, *and it is the one time an editor snipped something out of it. Without my knowledge. Now, it is in its original version, and I think I see what Ted meant. It strikes me as a weird story, and I've never done anything quite like it, before or since. But as for the whole acid–head bag — and by relation, pot and peyote and hash and mescalin and pill–dropping of all kinds — Ted's reportage of my attitude was precisely correct. Why should I clown around with all the artificial scenes when I've been on a continual high since the day I was born. I'll take my first fix or sugar cube when I come down, troops, but that may be a long way off if it is possible for me, unjugged, to write things like*

DELUSION FOR A
DRAGON SLAYER

This is true:

Chano Puzo, the incredibly talented conga drummer of the bop '40's, was inexplicably shot and killed by a beautiful Negress in the Rio Cafe, a Harlem bar, on December 2nd, 1948.

Dick Bong, pilot of a P–38 "Lightning" in World War Two, America's "Ace of Aces" with forty Japanese kills to his credit, who came through the hellfire of war unscratched, perished by accident when the jet engine of a Lockheed P–80 he was test–flying "flamed–out" and quit immediately after takeoff, August 7th, 1945. There was no reason for the mechanical failure, no reason for Bong to have died.

Marilyn Monroe, an extremely attractive young woman who had only recently begun to realize she possessed an acting ability far beyond that of "sex symbol" tagged on her early in her career, on a timeless and dateless day in 1962, left this life as a result of accidentally swallowing too many barbiturates. Despite lurid conjecture to the contrary, the evidence that she had been trying to phone someone for help as the tragedy coursed through her system, remains inescapable. It was an accident.

William Bolitho, one of the most incisive and miraculously talented commenters on society and its phychological motivations, whose "Murder For Profit" revolutionized psychiatric and penological attitudes toward the mentalities of mass–murderers, died suddenly—and again, tragically—in June of 1930, in a hospital in Avignon, victim of the mistaken judgment of an obscure French physician who let a simple case of appendicitis drop into peritonitis.

True.

Each of these four random deaths plucked from a staggering and nearly–endless compendium of "accidental tragedies" have one thing in common. With each other, and with the death of Warren Glazer Griffin. None of them should have happened. Each of them was "out–of–joint" with time and the continuity of the life in point. Each of them catches the breath, boggles the mind. Each of them could have been avoided, yet none of them could have been avoided. For each of them was pre–ordained. Not in the ethereal, mystic, supernatural flummery of the Kismet–believers, but in the complex rhythmic predestination of those who have been whisked out of their own world, into the mist–centuries of their dreams.

For Chano Puzo, it was a dark and smiling woman of mystery.

For Dick Bong, a winged Fury sent to find only him.

For Marilyn Monroe, a handful of white chalk pills.

For Bolitho, an inept quack forever doomed to apologies.

And for Warren Glazer Griffin, a forty–one year old accountant who, despite his advanced age, was still troubled by acne, and who never ventured further from his own world than Tenafly, New Jersey on a visit to relatives one June in 1959, it was a singular death ground to pulp between the triple–fanged rows of teeth in the mouth of a seventy–eight foot dragon, in a Land That Never Existed.

Wherein lies a biography, an historical footnote, a cautionary tale, and a keynote to the meaning of life.

Or, as Goethe summed it:

"Know thyself? If I knew myself, I'd run away."

The giant black "headache ball" of the wreckers struck the shell of a wall, and amid geysers of dust and powder and lath and plaster and brick and decayed wood, the third storey of the condemned office building crumbled, shivered along its width and imploded, plunging in upon itself, dumping jigsaw pieces into the hollow structure. The sound was a cannonade in the early–morning eight–o'clock street.

Forty years before, an obscure billionaire named Rouse, who had maintained a penthouse love–nest in the office building, in an unfashionable section of the city even then, had caused to be installed a private gas line to the kitchen of the flat; he was a lover of money, a lover of women, and a lover of flaming desserts. A private gas line. Gas company records of this installation had been either lost, destroyed, or—as seems more likely—carefully edited to exclude mention of the line. Graft, as well as bootlegging, had aided Rouse in his climb to that penthouse. The wreckers knew nothing of the gas line, which had long–since gone to disuse and the turnoff of a small valve on the third floor, which had originally jetted the vapor to the upper floor. Having no knowledge of the line, and having cleared all safety precautions with the city gas company as to existing installations, the wreckers hurled their destructive attentions at the third storey with assurance . . .

Warren Glazer Griffin left his home at precisely seven forty–five every weekday except Thursday (on which day he left at eight o'clock, to collect billing ledgers from his firm's other office, further downtown; an office which did not open till 8:15 weekdays). This was Thursday. He had run out of razor blades. That simple. He had had to pry a used blade out of the disposal niche in the blade container, and it had taken him ten minutes extra. He hurried and managed to leave the apartment house at 8:06 A.M. His routine was altered for the first time in seventeen years. That simple. Hurrying down the block to the Avenue, turning right and hesitating, realizing he could not make up the lost minutes by merely trotting (and without even recognizing the subliminal panic that gripped him at being off–schedule), he dashed across the Avenue, and cut through the little service alley running between the shopping mart, still closed, and the condemned office building with its high board fence constructed of thick doors from now–demolished offices . . .

U.S. WEATHER BUREAU FORECAST: partly cloudy today with a few scattered showers. Sunny and slightly warmer tomorrow (Friday). Gusty winds. High today 62. High Friday 60, low 43. Relative humidity . . .

Forty years past, a billionaire named Rouse.

A desire for flaming desserts.

A forgotten gas main.

A struggle for a used razor blade.

A short cut through an alley.

Gusty winds . . .

The "headache ball" plunged once more into the third storey, struck the bottled–up pressure valve; the entire side of the building erupted skyward on a spark struck by two bricks scratching together, ripping the massive iron sphere from its cable. The ball rose, arced, and borne on an unusually heavy wind, plummeted over the restraining board fence. It landed with a deafening crash in the alley.

Directly on the unsuspecting person of Warren Glazer Griffin, crushing him to little more than pulp, burying him eleven feet through cement and dirt and loam. Every building in the neighborhood shuddered at the impact.

And in several moments, cemetery silence fell once more in the chilly, eight–o–clock morning streets.

A soft, theremin humming, in little circles of sound, from all around him: the air was alive with multi–colored whispers of delight.

He opened his eyes and realized he was lying on the yellow–wood, highly–polished deck of a sailing vessel; to his left he could see beneath the rail a sea of purest vermillion, washing in thin lines of black and color, away behind the ship. Above him the silk and crystal sails billowed in the breeze, and tiny spheres of many–colored light kept pace with the vessel, as though they were lightning–bugs, sent to run convoy. He tried to stand up, and found it was not difficult: except he was now six feet three inches in height, not five foot seven.

Griffin looked down the length of his body, and for a suspended instant of eye–widening timelessness, he felt vertiginous. It was total displacement of ego. He was himself, and another himself entirely. He looked down, expecting to see a curved, pot–bellied and pimpled body he had worn for a very long time, but instead saw someone else, standing down below him, where he should have been. *Oh my God*, thought Warren Glazer Griffin, *I'm not me*.

The body that extended down to the polished deck was a fine instrument. Composed of the finest bronzed skin–tone, the most sculptured anthracite–hard musculature, proportions just the tiniest bit exaggerated, he was lovely and god–like, extremely god–like. Turning slowly, he caught his reflection in the burnished smoothness of a warrior's bronze shield, hung on a peg at the side of the forecastle. He was Nordic blond, aquiline–nosed, steely–blue–eyed. *No one can be that Aryan*, was his only thought, flushed with amazement, as he saw the new face molded to the front of his head.

He felt the hilt of the sword warm against his side.

He pulled it free of its scabbard, and stared in fascination at the face of the old, gnarled marmoset–eyed wizard whose countenance was an intaglio of pitted metal and jewels and sandblast–black briar, there engraved in hard relief on the handle. The face smiled gently at him.

"What it is all about, is this," the wizard said softly, so that not even the sea–birds careening overdecks would hear. "This is Heaven. But let me explain." Griffin had not considered an interruption. He was silent and struck dumb. "Heaven is what you mix all the days of your life, but you call it dreams. You have one chance to buy your Heaven with all the intents and ethics of your life. That is why everyone considers Heaven such a lovely place. Because it is dreams, special dreams, in which you exist. What you have to do is live up to them."

"I—" started Griffin, but the wizard cut him off with a rapid blinking of his strange eyes.

"No, listen, please, because after this, all the magic stops, and you have to do it alone.

"You create your own Heaven, and you have the opportunity to live in it, but you have to do it on your own terms, the highest terms of which you are capable. So sail this ship through the straits, navigate the shoals, find the island, overcome the foam–devil that guards the girl, win her love, and you've played the game on your own terms."

Then the wizard's face settled back into immobility, and Warren Glazer Griffin sat down heavily on the planking of the forecastle, mouth agape, eyes wide, and the realization of it all fixed firmly— unbelievably, but firmly—in his head.

Gee whiz, thought Griffin.

The sound of rigging shrieking like terns brought him out of his middle–class stupor, and he realized the keel of the strange and wonderful wind–vessel was coming about. The steady beatbeatbeat of pole–oars against mirror waters rose to meet the descending hum of a dying breeze, and the ship moved across reflective waters toward a mile–high breaker that abruptly rose out of the sea.

Griffin realized it had not leapt from the sea–bottom, as his first impression seemed to be, but had gradually grown on the horizon, some moments after the watch in the nest had halloo'd its imminent appearance. Yet he had not heard any such gardyloo; he was surfeited with thoughts of this other body, the golden god with the incredibly handsome face.

"Cap'n," said one of the hands, lumbering with sea legs toward him. "We're hard on the straits. Most of the men're shackled a'ready."

Griffin nodded silently, turned to follow the seaman. They moved back toward the lazzarette, and the seaman opened the hatch, dropped through. Griffin followed close behind him, and in the smallish compartment found the other sea–hands shackled wrists and ankles to the inner keel of the hold. He was gagged for a moment by the overpowering stench of salted bully–beef and fish, a sickly bittersweet smell that made his eyes smart with its intensity.

Then he moved to the seaman, who had already fastened his own ankle–shackles, and one wrist–manacle. He clapped the rusting manacle still undone, and now all the hands of the wind–vessel were locked immobile.

"Good luck, Cap'n," smiled the last seaman. And he winked. The other men joined in, in their own ways, with a dozen different accents, some in languages Griffin could not even begin to place. But all well–wishing. Griffin once more nodded in the strong, silent manner of someone other than himself, someone to the rank born.

Then he climbed out of the lazzarette and went aft to the wheel.

Overhead, the sky had darkened to a shining blackness, a patent leather black that would have sent back inverted reflections, had there been anything soaring close enough to the sky to reflect. In the mote–dancing waters of the ocean, a ghost ship sailed along upside–down, hull–to–hull with Griffin's vessel. And above him the quaint and tittering globes of light ricocheted and multiplied, filling the sudden night with the incense of their vibrancy. Their colors began to blend, to merge, to run down the sky in washes of color that made Griffin smile, and blink and drop his mouth open with awe. It was all the fireworks of another universe, just once hurled into an onyx sky, left to burn away whatever life was possible. Yet that was merely beginning:

The colors came. As he set his feet squarely, and the deltoids bunched furiously beneath his golden skin, the two men who were Warren Glazer Griffin began the complex water slalom that would send the vessel through the straits, past the shoals, and into the cove that lay beyond. And the colors came. The vessel tacked before the wind, which seemed to gather itself and enter in an arrowed spear pointed direction of unity, behind the massive sails. The wind was with him, sending him straight for the break in the heartless stone barrier. Out the colors game.

Softly at first, humming, creeping, boiling up from nowhere at the horizon line; twisting and surging like snake whirlwinds with adolescent intent; building, spiraling, climbing in vague streamers and tendrils of unconsciousness, the colors came.

In a rising, keening spiral of hysteria they came, first pulsing in primaries, then secondaries, the comminglings and off–shades, and finally in colors that had no names. Colors like racing, and pungent, and far seen shadows, and bitterness, and something that hurt, and something that pleasured. Oh, mostly the pleasures, one after another, singing, lulling, hypnotically arresting the eye as the ship sped into the heart of the maelstrom of weird, advancing, sky–eating colors. The siren colors of the straits. The colors that came from the air and the island and the world itself, which hushed and hurried across the world to here, to meet when they were needed, to stop the seamen who slid over the waves to the break in the breakwall. The colors, defense, that sent men to the bottom, their hearts bursting with songs of color and charm. The colors that top–filled a man to the brim and kept him poised there with a surface tension of joy and wonder, colors cascading like waterfalls of flowers in his head, millioncolors, blossomshades, brightnesses, joycrashing everythings that made a man hurl back and strain his throat to sing sing, sing chants of amazement and forever —

—as his ship plunged like a cannonball into the reefs and shattered into a billion wooden fragments, tiny splinters of dark wood against the boiling treacherous sea, and the rocks crushed and staved in the sides, and men's heads went to pulp as they hurtled forward and their vessel was cut out from under them, the colors the colors, the God beautiful colors!

As Griffin sang his song of triumph, the men with eyes clapped tightshut, belowdecks, saved from berserking, depending on this golden giant of a man who was their own personal this–trip God, who would bring them through the hole in the faceless evil rocks.

Griffin, singing!

Griffin, golden god from Manhattan!

Griffin, man of two skins, Chinese puzzle man within man, hands cross–locked over the wood of the wheel, tacking points this way, points that way, playing compass and swashbuckler with the deadly colors that lapped at his senses, filled his eyes with delight, clogged his nostrils with the scents of glory, all the tiny theremin hummings now merged, all the little color–motes now united, running in slippery washes down and down the sky as he hurried the vessel toward the rocks and then in one sweep as he spun spun spun the wheel two handed across, whip whip whip, and *through* into the bubbling white water, with rock–teeth screeching old women along the hull of his vessel, and tearing gouged gashes of darker deepness along the planking, but *through!*

Griffin, who chuckled with merriment at his grandeur, his stature, his chance taking, who had risked the lives of all his men for the moment of forever to be gained on that island. And winning! Making his wager with eternity, and winning—for an instant, before the great ship struck the buried reefs, and tore away the bottom of the ship, and the lazzarette filled in an instant, and his men who trusted him not to gamble them away so cheaply, wailed till their screams became water–logged, and were gone, and Griffin felt himself lifted, tossed, hurled, flung like a bit of suet and the thought that invaded, consumed, gnawed him in rage and frustration: that he had defeated the siren colors, had gotten through the treacherous straits, but had lost his men, his ship, even himself, by the treachery of his own self–esteem: that he had gloated over his wonderousness, and vanity had sent him whipping further inshore, to be dashed on reefs; and the bitterness welled in him as he struck the water with a paralyzing crash, and sank immediately beneath the boiling white–faced waves.

Out on the reefs, the wind–vessel, with its adamantine trim, with its onyx and alabaster sails, with its marvelous magical swiftness, sank beneath the waters without a murmur

(unless those silent insane shrieggggngggg wails were the sounds of men shackled helplessly to an open coffin) and all that could be heard was the pounding war drums of the waves, and the gutted, emptying, shrill keen of an animal whose throat has been slashed—the sound of the colors fading back to their million lairs around the universe, till they would be called again. Then after a while, even the waters smoothed.

Crickets gossiped shamelessly, close beside his head. He awoke to find his eyes open, staring up into a pale, cadaverous paper–thin cut–out that was the moon. Clouds scudding across its mottled slimness sent strange shadows washing across the night sky, the beach, the jungle, Warren Glazer Griffin.

Well, I certainly messed that up, was his first thought, and in an instant the thought was gone, and the Nordic god–man's thoughts superimposed more strenuously. Griffin felt his arms out wide on the white sand, and scraped them across the clinging grains till he was able to jack himself up, straining his back heavily. Propped on elbows, legs spread–eagled before him, he stared out to sea, to the great barrier wall that encircled the island, and scanned the dark expanse for some sign of ship or men. There was nothing. He let his mind linger for long moments on the vanity and ego that had cost so many lives.

Then he climbed painfully to his feet, and turned to look at the island. Jungle rose up in a thick tweedy tangle, as high as the consumptive moon, and the warp of dark vine tracery merged with a woof of sounds. Massed sounds, beasts, insects, night birds, unnameable sounds that chittered and rasped and howled and shrieked— even as his men had shrieked—and the scent–sounds of moist meat being ripped from the carcass of an ambushed soft creature was predominant. It was a living jungle, a presence in itself.

He pulled his sword, and struck off across the strand of white shadowed sand toward the rim edge of the tangle. In there somewhere, waited the girl, and the mist–devil, and the promise of life forever, here in this best of all possible worlds, his own Heaven, which he had made from a lifetime of dreams . . .

Yet the dream seemed relentlessly nightmarish, for the jungle resisted him, clawed at him, tempted yet rebuffed him. Griffin found himself hacking at the thick–fleshed twined and interwoven wall of foliage with growing ferocity. His even white teeth, beautifully matched and level, locked in a solid enamel band, and his eyes narrowed with frenzy. The hours melted into a shapeless colloid, and he could not tell whether he was making his way through the dense greenmass, or standing still while the jungle crawled imperceptibly toward him, filling in behind the clots he was hacking away. And darkness, suffocating, in the jungle.

Abruptly, he lunged forward against a singularly rugged matting of interlocked tree branches and hurled himself through the break, as it fell away, unresisting. He was in the clear. At the top of a rise that sloped away below him in softly–curved smoothness, toward a rushing stream of gently–whispering white water. Around small stones it raced, gathering speed, a gentle moist animal streaking toward a far land.

Griffin found himself loping down the hill, toward the bank of the stream, and as he ran, his body grew more and more his own. The hill grew up behind him, and the stream came toward him with gentleness, and he was there: time was another thing here, not forced, not necessary, a pastel passage, without hard edges.

He followed the stream, skirting banks of thickets and trees that seemed to be windswept in their topmost branches, and the stream became a river, and the river rushed to rapids, and then suddenly there were falls. Not great thundering falls down which men might be swept in fragile canoes, but murmuring ledges and sweeps down which the white water surged sweetly, carrying tinges of color from the banks, carrying vagrant leaves and blades of grass, gently, tenderly, comfortingly. Griffin stood silently, watching the waterfall, sensing more than he saw, understanding more than even his senses could tell him. This was, indeed, the Heaven of his dreams, a place to spend the rest of forever, with the wind and the water and the world another place, another level of sensing, another bad dream had many long times before. This was reality, an only reality for a man whose existence had been not quite bad, merely insufficient; tenable, but hardly enriching. For a man who had lived a life of not quite enough, this was all that there ever could be of goodness and brilliance and light. Griffin moved toward the falls.

The darkness grew darker.

Glowing in the dimensionless whispering dimness, Griffin saw a scene that could only have come from his dreams. The girl, naked white against the ledges and slopes of the falls, water cascading down her back, across her thighs, cool against her belly, her head laid back and white water bubbling through the shining black veil of her hair, touching each strand, silkily shining it with moisture; her eyes closed in simple pleasure; that face, the *right* face, the special face, the certain face of the woman he had always looked for without looking, hunted silently for, without acknowledging the search; lusted for, without feeling worthy of the hunger.

It was the woman his finest instincts had needed to make them valid; the woman who not only gave to him, but to whom he could give; the woman of memory, of desire, of youth, of restlessness, of completion. A dream. And here, against the softspeaking bubbling water, a reality. Glowing magically in the night, the girl raised a hand languidly and with joy, simple unspoken joy, and Griffin started toward her as the mist–devil materialized. Out of the foam spray, out of the night, out of the suddenly rising chill fog and vapor and cloud–slime, out of starshine and evil mists without proper names, the devil that guarded this woman of visions, materialized. Giant, gigantic, massive, rising higher and higher, larger, more intensely defined against nightness, the devil spread across the sky in a towering, smooth–edged reality.

Great sad eyes, the white molten centers of rat holes in which whirlwinds lived. A brow: massive leaded furrows drawing down in unctuous pleasure at sight of the girl, creature this horrendous, creature this gigantic, liaison with white flesh? The thought skittered like a poisoned rodent across the floor of Griffin's mind, like a small creature with one leg torn off, pain and blood–red ganglia of conception, then lost itself in the bittersweet crypt beneath thoughts: too repugnant, too monstrous for continued examination. And the mist–devil rose and rose and expanded, and bellows–blew its chest to horizon–filling proportions. Griffin fell back into shadows lest he be seen.

More, greater, still more massive it rose, filling the night sky till it obscured the moon, till nightbirds lived in its face, till molten tremblings—the very stars—served it as exhalations of breath. The mouth of a maniac millions magnified, was its mouth. Terror and fear and whimperings from far underground were the lines of character in a face incalculably old, ancient, decayed with a time that could not be called time by men. And it was one with this woman. It consorted, filthy liaison, subliminal haunted pleiocene gonadal urgings, it and woman, force incarnate and gentle labial moistures. This: the terrible end–hunger of a million billion eons of forced abstinence.

The forever paramour, the eternity lecher, the consumed–by–desire that rose and rose and blotted the world with its bulk. The mist–devil Warren Glazer Griffin had to kill, before he could live forever in his dreams.

Griffin stood back in shadows, trembling within the golden body he wore. Now, abruptly, he was two men once again. The god with his sword, the mortal with his fear. And he swore to himself that he could not do it, could not—even crying inside that poor glorious shell—and could not, and was terribly afraid. But then, as he watched, the mist–devil seemed to implode, drew in upon himself, shrinking shrinking shrinking down and down and down into a smaller tighter neater less infinitely tinier replica of himself, like a gas–filled balloon suddenly released from the hand of a child, whipping, snapping, spinning through the air growing smaller as it lost its muscled tautness . . .

And the mist–devil became the size of a man.

And it went to the woman.

And they made love.

Griffin watched in disgust and loathing as the creature that was age, that was night, that was fear, that was everything save the word *human*, placed hands on white breasts, placed lips on pliant red mouth, placed thighs around belly, and the woman's arms came up, and embraced the creature of always, and they locked in twisting union, there in the white bubbling water, with the stars shrieking overhead and the moon a bloating madness careening down a sinkhole of space, as Warren Glazer Griffin watched the woman of all his thoughts take in the manhood of something anything but man. And silently, like a footpad, Griffin crept up behind the devil of mist, locked in trembling consumation of desire, and linking his wet and sticky hands about the hilt of the weapon, he raised it up over his head, spread–legged like an executioner, and drove the blade viciously, but at an angle, downdowndown and with the thickrasping crunch of metal through meat, into and out the other side of the neck of the creature.

It drew in a hideous world–load of air, gasping it up and into torn flesh, a rattling distended neck–straining blowfish mass of air, that ended with a sound so high and pathetic that skin prickled up and down Griffin's cheeks, his neck, his back, and the monstrous creature reached off to nowhere to pull out the insane iron that had destroyed him, and the hand went to another location, and the blade was ripped free by Griffin, as the devil rose off the woman, dripping blood and dripping the fluid of love and dripping life away in every instant, careening into the falls with deadfish stains of all–colored blood in the wake, and turned once, to stare full into Griffin's face with a look that denounced him:

From behind!

From behind!

Was gone. Was dead. Was floated down waterfalls to deep stygian pools of refuse and rubble and rust. To silt bottoms where nothing mattered, but gone.

Leaving Warren Glazer Griffin to stand with blood that had spurted up across his wide golden chest, staring down at the woman of his dreams, whose eyes were cataracted with frenzy and fear. All the dream orgies of his life, all the wild couplings of his adolescent nightmares, all the wants and hungers and needs of his woman sensings, were here.

The girl gave only one shrill howl before he took her. He had thoughts all during the frantic struggle and just at the penetration: womanwhore slutlover trollopmine over and over and over and over and when he rose from her, the eyes that stared back at him, like leaves in snow, on the first day of winter. Empty winds howled down out of the tundras of his soul. This was the charnel house of his finest fantasies. The burial ground of his forever. The garbage dump, the slain meat, the putrefying reality of his dreams and his Heaven.

Griffin stumbled away from her, hearing the shrieks of men needlessly drowned by his vanity, hearing the voiceless accusation of the devil proclaiming cowardice, hearing the orgasm–condemnation of lust that was never love, of brute desire that was never affection, and realizing at last that these were the real substances of his nature, the true faces of his sins, the marks in the ledger of a life he had never led, yet had worshipped silently at an altar of evil.

All these thoughts, as the guardian of Heaven, the keeper at the gate, the claimer of souls, the weigher of balances, advanced on him through the night.

Griffin looked up and had but a moment to realize he had not succeeded in winning his Heaven . . . as the seventy–eight–foot creature he could have called nothing less than a dragon opened its mouth that was all the world and judgment, and ground him to senseless pulp between rows of triple–fanged teeth.

When they dug the body out of the alley, it made even the hardened construction workers and emergency squad cops ill. Not one bone was left unbroken. The very flesh seemed to have been masticated as if by a nation of cannibal dogs. Even so, the three innured excavators who finally used winding sheets and shovels to bring the shapeless mass up from its eleven foot grave, agreed that it was incredible, totally passed belief, that the head and face were untouched.

And they all agreed that the expression *on* the face was not one of happiness. There were many possible explanations for that expression, but none of them would have said terror, for it was not terror. They would not have said helplessness, for it was not that, either. They might have settled on a pathetic sense of loss, had their sensibilities run that deep, but none of them would have felt that the expression said, with great finality: a man may truly live in his dreams, his noblest dreams, but only, *only* if he is worthy of those dreams.

It did not rain that night, anywhere in the known universe.

This is the end of the book. One of my favorite stories. Also, the last introduction. Peculiar thing about these introductions: they began as simply random notes on theme in my first collection. Then, as the years have passed, they have become more and more important, more integrated with what I've been trying to say in my fiction. The response to them is mixed. There are reviewers and critics and fans who think the stories should be thrown out, and the introductions kept; perhaps an entire book of bibble–bibble–bibble. There is another faction that hates me so much personally, they cannot stand the intrusion of my personality. The stories they don't seem to mind much (though they contend I'm a poor lousy hack with a tiny gift for explosiveness). But the intros drive them cockeyed. They pray that either I stop writing prefaces, or lightning strikes me in the spleen. There are some who enjoy the totality, who think they get more for their money and their enjoyment with this additional material specially–written for a book. And there are the vast multitudes who think the entire item ought to be burned as it comes off the presses. There are even a couple of people in Pocatello who've never heard of me, but mostly, they just stand around looking at the sky hoping to see another of them great silver birds go fly–fly to the sunset. Suffice it to say, I enjoy writing these little writer–to–reader liaisons, so get used to it, troops. Relief is nowhere in sight. But sometimes the background of a story is almost more interesting than the yarn I made from it. Take this story, for instance. Maggie lives! She is a tall blonde in Los Angeles. I never quite got her into bed, though it was close. I had dated her sporadically, for a year or so, back in 1963, and then lost track of her. Then, when Joseph E. Levine flew the cast and production people of "The Oscar" to Las Vegas for Tony Bennett's opening at The Riviera, in conjunction with the film in which Tony was appearing, I met her again. It was very late. Everybody else had either gone to bed, or picked up some action, or were gambling. I was sitting alone at the blackjack table, in my tuxedo, when a hand was laid on my shoulder. I turned around and it was —whooops. I almost called her by her real name. It was Maggie. She was in the chorus line at one of the hotels, and I suspect she was hooking on the side. We talked and she invited me home with her. But it stirred up all sorts of remembrances of the chick, and most particularly the bedroom and bathroom of her apartment in Los Angeles. Strange that I would think of that, at that moment, but I remembered vividly walking into the bedroom the first time I came to pick *her up. Everything was plush red velvet, like a New Orleans whorehouse. The bathroom fixtures were gold dolphins spewing out water. There was a frantic need to be elegant for this girl. She had come from simple beginnings, and "class" was her goal in this life. Somehow, seeing her again in Vegas, she fitted the town more precisely than anyone else I'd ever met. I hate Vegas. It represents a physical manifestation of evil in this country, for my money. (None of which I lose at the tables, incidentally; I'm phenomenally lucky.) But she fit. Not that she was evil, just that she was right for the town... a product of the times. So I suddenly had the alarming experience of my intellect getting the better of my gonads, and I turned down her offer of bed-service, because all at once, in a total presence of structure, the story that follows popped into my head. I bid her a suave adieu and dashed up to my room in The Riviera. I had my typewriter with me. I always have my typewriter with me, I stripped down naked (which is the way I write frequently) and started writing the story. Between getting dressed and dashing downstairs to bug the casino manager for facts and specifics on slot machines (and incidentally, everything in this story is accurate), and sitting directly in the line of the air conditioning, by morning the story was half-finished and I had pleurisy. I went into a coma later that day, and they had to fly my unconscious carcass back to LA, where I went into a hospital, When I got out, I finished the yarn. I have seen "Maggie" several times since, but by now she is so firmly entrenched in my thinking as the character of the story, that I could no more bring myself to lay her than I could to re-visit Vegas. Both are deadly, and the further away from each of them I stay, the better. A note on style, before I go. I've tried in this story to give a sense of the immediacy, the whambangthankyoumaam of Vegas. The style I've employed is pure concussion. But I scream helplessly at the inadequacies of the lineal medium. There is a section herein, in which I try to convey a sense of impression of the moment of death. In films I could use effects. In type-on-paper it comes down to the enormously ineffectual italics, type tricks, staccato sentences and spacings of a man groping to expand his medium. Bear with me. It is experimentation, and unless typesetters and editors somehow develop the miracle talent of letting writers tear the form apart, to reassemble it in their individual ways, the best I'll be able to do in terms of freedom of impact is what I got away with here in*

PRETTY MAGGIE MONEYEYES

With an eight hole–card and a queen showing, with the dealer showing a four up, Kostner decided to let the house do the work. So he stood, and the dealer turned up. Six.

The dealer looked like something out of a 1935 George Raft film: Arctic diamond–chip eyes, manicured fingers long as a brain surgeon's, straight black hair slicked flat away from the pale forehead. He did not look up as he peeled them off. A three. Another three. Bam. A five. Bam. Twenty–one, and Kostner saw his last thirty dollars—six five–dollar chips—scraped on the edge of the cards, into the dealer's chip racks. Busted. Flat. Down and out in Las Vegas, Nevada. Playground of the Western World.

He slid off the comfortable stool–chair and turned his back on the blackjack table. The action was already starting again, like waves closing over a drowned man. He had been there, was gone, and no one had noticed. No one had seen a man blow the last tie with salvation. Kostner now had his choice: he could bum his way into Los Angeles and try to find something that resembled a new life . . . or he could go blow his brains out through the back of his head.

Neither choice showed much light or sense.

He thrust his hands deep into the pockets of his worn and dirty chinos, and started away down the line of slot machines clanging and rattling on the other side of the aisle between blackjack tables.

He stopped. He felt something in his pocket. Beside him, but all-engrossed, a fiftyish matron in electric lavender capris, high heels and Ship n' Shore blouse was working two slots, loading and pulling one while waiting for the other to clock down. She was dumping quarters in a seemingly inexhaustible supply from a Dixie cup held in her left hand. There was a surrealistic presence to the woman. She was almost automated, not a flicker of expression on her face, the eyes fixed and unwavering. Only when the gong rang, someone down the line had pulled a jackpot, did she look up. And at that moment Kostner knew what was wrong and immoral and deadly about Vegas, about legalized gambling, about setting the traps all baited and open in front of the average human. The woman's face was gray with hatred, envy, lust and dedication to the game—in that timeless instant when she heard another drugged soul down the line winning a minuscule jackpot. A jackpot that would only lull the player with words like *luck* and *ahead of the game*. The jackpot lure: the sparkling, bobbling many–colored wiggler in a sea of poor fish.

The thing in Kostner's pocket was a silver dollar.

He brought it out and looked at it.

The eagle was hysterical.

But Kostner pulled to an abrupt halt, only one half–footstep from the sign indicating the limits of Tap City. He was still with it. What the high–rollers called the edge, the *vigerish*, the fine hole–card. One buck. One cartwheel. Pulled out of the pocket not half as deep as the pit into which Kostner had just been about to plunge.

What the hell, he thought, and turned to the row of slot machines.

He had thought they'd all been pulled out of service, the silver dollar slots. A shortage of coinage, said the United States Mint. But right there, side by side with the nickel and quarter bandits, was one cartwheel machine. Two thousand dollar jackpot. Kostner grinned foolishly. If you're gonna go out, go out like a champ.

He thumbed the silver dollar into the coin slot and grabbed the heavy, oiled handle. Shining cast aluminum and pressed steel. Big black plastic ball, angled for arm–ease, pull it all day and you won't get weary.

Without a prayer in the universe, Kostner pulled the handle.

She had been born in Tucson, mother full–blooded Cherokee, father a bindlestiff on his way through. Mother had been working a truckers' stop, father had popped for spencer steak and sides. Mother had just gotten over a bad scene, indeterminate origins, unsatisfactory culminations. Mother had popped for bed. And sides. Margaret Annie Jessie had come nine months later; black of hair, fair of face, and born into a life of poverty. Twenty–three years later, a determined product of Miss Clairol and Berlitz, a dream–image formed by Vogue and intimate association with the rat race, Margaret Annie Jessie had become a contraction.

Maggie.

Long legs, trim and coltish; hips a trifle large, the kind that promote that specific thought in men, about getting their hands around it; belly flat, isometrics; waist cut to the bone, a waist that works in any style from dirndl to disco–slacks; no breasts—all nipple, but no breast, like an expensive whore (the way O'Hara pinned it)—and no padding . . . forget the cans, baby, there's other, more important action; smooth, Michelangelo–sculpted neck, a pillar, proud; and all that face.

Outthrust chin, perhaps a tot too much belligerence, but if you'd walloped as many gropers, you too, sweetheart; narrow mouth, petulant lower lip, nice to chew on, a lower lip as though filled with honey, bursting, ready for things to happen; a nose that threw the right sort of shadow, flaring nostrils, the acceptable words—aquiline, patrician, classic, allathat; cheekbones as stark and promontory as a spit of land after ten years of open ocean; cheekbones holding darkness like narrow shadows, sooty beneath the taut–fleshed bone-structure; amazing cheekbones, the whole face, really; simple uptilted eyes, the touch of the Cherokee, eyes that looked out at you, as you looked in at them, like someone peering out of the keyhole as you peered in; actually, dirty eyes, they said you can get it.

Blonde hair, a great deal of it, wound and rolled and smoothed and flowing, in the old style, the pageboy thing men always admire; no tight little cap of slicked plastic; no ratted and teased Anapurna of bizarre coiffure; no ironed–flat discothèque hair like number 3 flat noodles. Hair, the way a man wants it, so he can dig his hands in at the base of the neck and pull all that face very close.

An operable woman, a working mechanism, a rigged and sudden machinery of softness and motivation.

Twenty–three, and determined as hell never to abide in that vale of poverty her mother had called purgatory for her entire life; snuffed out in a grease fire in the last trailer, somewhere in Arizona, thank God no more pleas for a little money from babygirl Maggie hustling drinks in a Los Angeles topless joint. (There ought to be some remorse in there somewhere, for a Mommy gone where all the good grease–fire victims go. Look around, you'll find it.)

Maggie.

Genetic freak. Mommy's Cherokee uptilted eye–shape, and Polack quick-screwing Daddy WithoutaName's blue as innocence color.

Blue–eyed Maggie, dyed blonde, alla that face, alla that leg, fifty bucks a night can get it and it sounds *like it's having a climax.*

Irish–innocent blue–eyed innocent French–legged innocent Maggie. Polack. Cherokee. Irish. All–woman and going on the market for this month's rent on the stucco pad, eighty bucks' worth of groceries, a couple month's worth for a Mustang, three appointments with the specialist in Beverly Hills about that shortness of breath after a night on the hustle bump the sticky thigh the disco lurch the gotcha sweat: woman minutes. Increments under the meat; perspiration purchases, yeah it does.

Maggie, Maggie, Maggie, pretty Maggie Moneyeyes, who came from Tucson and trailers and rheumatic fever and a surge to live that was all kaleidoscope frenzy of clawing scrabbling no–nonsense. If it took laying on one's back and making sounds like a panther in the desert, then one did it, because nothing, but nothing was as bad as being dirt–poor, itchy–skinned, soiled–underwear, scuff–toed, hairy and ashamed lousy with the no–gots. Nothing!

Maggie. Hooker. Hustler. Grabber. Swinger. If there's a buck in it, there's rhythm and the onomatopoeia is Maggie Maggie Maggie.

She who puts out. For a price, whatever that might be.

Maggie was dating Nuncio. He was Sicilian. He had dark eyes and an alligator–grain wallet with slip–in pockets for credit cards. He was a spender, a sport, a high–roller. They went to Vegas.

Maggie and the Sicilian. Her blue eyes and his slip–in pockets. But mostly her blue eyes.

The spinning reels behind the three long glass windows blurred, and Kostner knew there wasn't a chance. Two thousand dollar jack-pot. Round and round, whirring. Three bells or two bells and a jackpot bar, get 18; three plums or two plums and a jackpot bar, get 14; three oranges or two oranges and a jac —

Ten, five, two bucks for a single cherry cluster in first position. Something . . . I'm drowning . . . something . . .

The whirring . . .

Round and round . . .

As something happened that was not considered in the pit–boss manual.

The reels whipped and snapped to a stop, clank clank clank, tight in place.

Three bars looked up at Kostner. But they did not say JACKPOT. They were three bars on which stared three blue eyes. Very blue, very immediate, very JACKPOT!!

Twenty silver dollars clattered into the payoff trough at the bottom of the machine. An orange light popped on in the Casino Cashier's cage, bright orange on the jackpot board. And the gong began clanging overhead.

The Slot Machine Floor Manager nodded once to the Pit Boss, who pursed his lips and started toward the seedy–looking man still standing with his hand on the slot's handle.

The token payment—twenty silver dollars—lay untouched in the payoff trough. The balance of the jackpot—one thousand nine hundred and eighty dollars—would be paid manually by the Casino Cashier. And Kostner stood, dumbly, as the three blue eyes stared up at him.

There was a moment of idiotic disorientation, as Kostner stared back at the three blue eyes; a moment in which the slot machine's mechanisms registered to themselves; and the gong was clanging furiously.

All through the hotel's Casino people turned from their games to stare. At the roulette tables the white–on–white players from Detroit and Cleveland pulled their watery eyes away from the clattering ball and stared down the line for a second, at the ratty–looking guy in front of the slot machine. From where they sat, they could not tell it was a two grand pot, and their rheumy eyes went back into billows of cigar smoke, and that little ball.

The blackjack hustlers turned momentarily, screwing around in their seats, and smiled. They were closer to the slot–players in temperament, but they knew the slots were a dodge to keep the old ladies busy, while the players worked toward their endless twenty–ones.

And the old dealer, who could no longer cut it at the fast–action boards, who had been put out to pasture by a grateful management, standing at the Wheel of Fortune near the entrance to the Casino, even he paused in his zombie–murmuring ("Annnnother winner onna Wheel of Forchun!") to no one at all, and looked toward Kostner and that incredible gong–clanging. Then, in a moment, still with no players, he called *another* nonexistent winner.

Kostner heard the gong from far away. It had to mean he had won two thousand dollars, but that was impossible. He checked the payoff chart on the face of the machine. Three bars labeled JACKPOT meant JACKPOT. Two thousand dollars.

But these three bars did not say JACKPOT. They were three gray bars, rectangular in shape, with a blue eye directly in the center of each bar.

Blue eyes?

Somewhere, a connection was made, and electricity, a billion volts of electricity, were shot through Kostner. His hair stood on end, his fingertips bled raw, his eyes turned to jelly, and every fiber in his musculature became radioactive. Somewhere, out there, in a place that was not this *place, Kostner had been inextricably bound to — to someone. Blue eyes?*

The gong had faded out of his head, the constant noise level of the Casino, chips chittering, people mumbling, dealers calling plays, it had all gone, and he was embedded in silence.

Tied to that someone else, out there somewhere, through those three blue eyes.

Then in an instant, it had passed, and he was alone again, as though released by a giant hand, the breath crushed out of him. He staggered up against the slot machine.

"You all right, fellah?"

A hand gripped him by the arm, steadied him. The gong was still clanging overhead somewhere, and he was breathless from a journey he had just taken. His eyes focused and he found himself looking at the stocky Pit Boss who had been on duty while he had been playing blackjack.

"Yeah . . . I'm okay, just a little dizzy is all."

"Sounds like you got yourself a big jackpot, fellah," the Pit Boss grinned. It was a leathery grin; something composed of stretched muscles and conditioned reflexes, totally mirthless.

"Yeah . . . great . . . " Kostner tried to grin back. But he was still shaking from that electrical absorption that had kidnaped him.

"Let me check it out," the Pit Boss was saying, edging around Kostner, and staring at the face of the slot machine. "Yeah, three jackpot bars, all right. You're a winner."

Then it dawned on Kostner! Two thousand dollars! He looked down at the slot machine and saw —

Three bars with the word JACKPOT on them. No blue eyes, just words that meant money. Kostner looked around frantically, was he losing his mind? *From somewhere, not in the Casino room, he heard a tinkle of rhodium–plated laughter.*

He scooped up the twenty silver dollars. The Pit Boss dropped another cartwheel into the Chief, and pulled the jackpot off. Then the Pit Boss walked him to the rear of the Casino, talking to him in a muted, extremely polite tone of voice. At the Cashier's window, the Pit Boss nodded to a weary–looking man at a huge Rolodex card–file, checking credit ratings.

"Barney, jackpot on the cartwheel Chief; slot five–oh–oh–one–five." He grinned at Kostner, who tried to smile back. It was difficult. He felt stunned.

The Cashier checked a payoff book for the correct amount to be drawn and leaned over the counter toward Kostner. "Check or cash, sir?"

Kostner felt buoyancy coming back to him. "Is the Casino's check good?" They all three laughed at that. "A check's fine," Kostner said. The check was drawn, and the Check–Riter punched out the little bumps that said two thousand. "The twenty chartwheels are a gift," the Cashier said, sliding the check through to Kostner.

He held it, looked at it, and still found it difficult to believe. Two grand, back on the golden road.

As he walked back through the Casino with the Pit Boss, the stocky man asked pleasantly, "Well, what are you going to do with it?" Kostner had to think a moment. He didn't really have any plans. But then the sudden realization came to him: "I'm going to play that slot machine again." The Pit Boss smiled: a congenital sucker. He would put all twenty of those silver dollars back into the Chief, and then turn to the other games. Blackjack, roulette, faro, baccarat . . . in a few hours he would have redeposited the two grand with the hotel Casino. It always happened.

He walked Kostner back to the slot machine, and patted him on the shoulder. "Lotsa luck, fellah."

As he turned away, Kostner slipped a silver dollar into the machine, and pulled the handle.

The Pit Boss had only taken five steps when he heard the incredible sound of the reels clicking to a stop, the clash of twenty token silver dollars hitting the payoff trough, and that goddammed gong went out of its mind again.

She had known that sonofabitch Nuncio was a perverted swine. A walking filth. A dungheap between his ears. Some kind of monster in nylon undershorts. There weren't many kinds of games Maggie hadn't played, but what that Sicilian De Sade wanted to do was outright vomity!

She nearly fainted when he suggested it. Her heart—which the Beverly Hills specialist had said she should not tax—began whumping frantically. "You pig!" she screamed. "You filthy dirty ugly pig you, Nuncio you pig!" She had bounded out of the bed and started to throw on clothes. She didn't even bother with a brassiere, pulling the poorboy sweater on over her thin breasts, still crimson with the touches and love–bites Nuncio had showered on them.

He sat up in the bed, a pathetic–looking little man, gray hair at the temples and no hair atall on top, and his eyes were moist. He was porcine, was indeed the swine she called him, but he was helpless before her. He was in love with his hooker, with the tart whom he was supporting. It had been the first time for the swine Nuncio, and he was helpless. Back in Detroit, had it been a floozy, a chippy broad, he would have gotten out of the double bed and rapped her around pretty good. But this Maggie, she tied him in knots. He had suggested . . . that, what they should do together . . . because he was so consumed with her. But she was furious with him. It wasn't that bizarre an idea!

"Gimme a chanct'a talk t'ya, honey . . . Maggie . . . "

"You filthy pig, Nuncio! Give me some money, I'm going down to the Casino, and I don't want to see your filthy pig face for the rest of the day, remember that!"

And she had gone in his wallet and pants, and taken eight hundred and sixteen dollars, while he watched. He was helpless before her. She was something stolen from a world he knew only as "class" and she could do what she wanted with him.

Genetic freak Maggie, blue–eyed posing mannequin Maggie, pretty Maggie Moneyeyes, who was one–half Cherokee and one–half a buncha other things, had absorbed her lessons well. She was the very model of a "class broad."

"Not for the rest of the day, do you understand?" she snapped at him, and went downstairs, furious, to fret and gamble and wonder about nothing but years of herself.

Men stared after her as she walked. She carried herself like a challenge, the way a squire carried a pennant, the way a prize bitch carried herself in the judge's ring. Born to the blue. The wonders of mimicry and desire.

Maggie had no lust for gambling, none whatever. She merely wanted to taste the fury of her relationship with the swine Sicilian, her need for solidarity in a life built on the edge of the slide area, the senselessness of being here in Las Vegas when she could be back in Beverly Hills. She grew angrier and more ill at the thought of Nuncio upstairs in the room, taking another shower. She bathed three times a day. But it was different with him. He knew she resented his smell; he had the soft odor of wet fur sometimes, and she had told him about it. Now he bathed constantly, and hated it. He was a foreigner to the bath. His life had been marked by various kinds of filths, and baths for him now were more of an obscenity than dirt could ever have been. For her, bathing was different. It was a necessity. She had to keep the patina of the world off her, had to remain clean and smooth and white. A presentation, not an object of flesh and hair. A chromium instrument, something never pitted by rust and corrosion.

When she was touched by them, by any one of them, by the men, by all the Nuncios, they left little pitholes of bloody rust on her white, permanent flesh; cobwebs, sooty stains. She had to bathe. Often.

She strolled down between the tables and the slots, carrying eight hundred and sixteen dollars. Eight one hundred dollar bills and sixteen dollars in ones.

At the change booth she got cartwheels for the sixteen ones. The Chief waited. It was her baby. She played it to infuriate the Sicilian. He had told her to play the nickle slots, the quarter or dime slots, but she always infuriated him by blowing fifty or a hundred dollars in ten minutes, one coin after another, in the big Chief.

She faced the machine squarely, and put in the first silver dollar. She pulled the handle that swine Nuncio. Another dollar, pulled the handle how long does this go on? The reels cycled and spun and whirled and whipped in a blurringspinning metalhumming overandoverandover as Maggie blue-eyed Maggie hated and hated and thought of hate and all the days and nights of swine behind her and ahead of her and if only she had all the money in this room in this Casino in this hotel in this town right now this very instant just an instant thisinstant it would be enough to whirring and humming *and spinning and overandoverandoverandover and she would be free free free and all the world would never touch her body again the swine would never touch her white flesh again and then suddenly as dollarafterdollarafterdollar went aroundaroundaround hummmmming in reels of cherries and bells and bars and plums and oranges there was suddenly painpainpain a SHARP pain!pain!pain! in her chest, her heart, her center, a needle, a lancet, a burning, a pillar of flame that was purest pure purer PAIN!*

Maggie, pretty Maggie Moneyeyes, who wanted all that money in that cartwheel Chief slot machine, Maggie who had come from filth and rheumatic fever, who had come all the way to three baths a day and a specialist in Very Expensive Beverly Hills, that Maggie suddenly had a seizure, a flutter, a slam of a coronary thrombosis and fell instantly dead on the floor of the Casino. Dead.

One instant she had been holding the handle of the slot machine, willing her entire being, all that hatred for all the swine she had ever rolled with, willing every fiber of every cell of every chromosome into that machine, wanting to suck out every silver vapor within its belly, and the next instant—so close they might have been the same—her heart exploded and killed her and she slipped to the floor . . . still touching the Chief.

On the floor.
Dead.
Struck dead.
Liar. All the lies that were her life.
Dead on a floor.

[A moment out of time • lights whirling and spinning in a cotton candy universe • down a bottomless funnel roundly sectioned like a goat's horn • a cornucopia that rose up cuculiform smooth and slick as a worm belly • endless nights that pealed ebony funeral bells • out of fog • out of weightlessness • suddenly total cellular knowledge • memory running backward • gibbering spastic blindness • a soundless owl of frenzy trapped in a cave of prisms • sand endlessly draining down • billows of forever • edges of the world as they splintered • foam rising drowning from inside • the smell of rust • rough green corners that burn • memory the gibbering spastic blind memory • seven rushing vacuums of nothing • yellow • pinpoints cast in amber straining and elongating running like live wax • chill fevers •

overhead the odor of stop • this is the stopover before hell or heaven • this is limbo • trapped and doomed alone in a mist–eaten nowhere • a soundless screaming a soundless whirring a soundless spinning spinning spinning • spinning • spinning • spinning • spinning • spinninggggggggggggggggg]

> Maggie had wanted all the silver in the machine. She had died, willing herself into the machine. Now looking out from within, from inside the limbo that had become her own purgatory, Maggie was trapped, in the oiled and anodize interior of the silver dollar slot machine. The prison of her final desires, where she had wanted to be, completely trapped in that last instant of life between life/death. Maggie, gone inside; all soul now; trapped for eternity in the cage soul of the soulless machine. Limbo. Trapped.

"I hope you don't mind if I call over one of the slot men," the Slot Machine Floor Manager was saying, from a far distance. He was in his late fifties, a velvet–voiced man whose eyes held nothing of light and certainly nothing of kindness. He had stopped the Pit Boss as the stocky man had turned in mid–step to return to Kostner and the jackpotted machine; he had taken the walk himself. "We have to make sure, you know how it is, somebody didn't fool the slot, you know, maybe it's outta whack or something, you know."

He lifted his left hand and there was a clicker in it, the kind children use at Halloween. He clicked half a dozen times, like a rabid cricket, and there was a scurrying in the pit between the tables.

Kostner was only faintly aware of what was happening. Instead of being totally awake, feeling the surge of adrenaline through his veins, the feeling any gambler gets when he is ahead of the game, a kind of desperate urgency when he has hit it for a boodle, he was numb, partaking of the action around him only as much as a drinking glass involves itself in the alcoholic's drunken binge.

All color and sound had been leached out of him.

A tired–looking, resigned–weary man wearing a gray porter's jacket, as gray as his hair, as gray as his indoor skin, came to them, carrying a leather wrap–up of tools. The slot repairman studied the machine, turning the pressed steel body around on its stand, studying the back. He used a key on the back door and for an instant Kostner had a view of gears, springs, armatures and the clock that ran the slot mechanism. The repairman nodded silently over it, closed and relocked it, turned it around again and studied the face of the machine.

"Nobody's been spooning it," he said, and went away.

Kostner stared at the Floor Manager.

"Gaffing. That's what he meant. Spooning's another word for it. Some guys use a little piece of plastic, or a wire, shove it down through the escalator, it kicks the machine. Nobody thought that's what happened here, but you know, we have to make sure, two grand is a big payoff, and twice . . . well, you know, I'm sure you'll understand. If a guy was doing it with a boomerang—"

Kostner raised an eyebrow.

"—uh, yeah, a boomerang, it's another way to spoon the machine. But we just wanted to make a little check, and now everybody's satisfied, so if you'll just come back to the Casino Cashier with me—"

And they paid him off again.

So he went back to the slot machine, and stood before it for a long time, staring at it. The change girls and the dealers going off–duty; the little old ladies with their canvas work gloves worn to avoid calluses when pulling the slot handles, the men's room attendant on his way up front to get more matchbooks, the floral tourists, the idle observers, the hard drinkers, the sweepers, the busboys, the gamblers with poached–egg eyes who had been up all night, the showgirls with massive breasts and diminutive sugar daddies, all of them conjectured mentally about the beat–up walker who was staring at the silver dollar Chief. He did not move, merely stared at the machine . . . and they wondered.

The machine was staring back at Kostner.

Three blue eyes.

The electric current had sparked through him again, as the machine had clocked down and the eyes turned up a second time, as he had *won* a second time. But this time he knew there was something more than luck involved, for no one else had seen those three blue eyes.

So now he stood before the machine, waiting. It spoke to him. Inside his skull, where no one had ever lived but himself, now someone else moved and spoke to him. A girl. A beautiful girl. Her name was Maggie, and she spoke to him.

I've been waiting for you. A long time, I've been waiting for you, Kostner. Why do you think you hit the jackpot? Because I've been waiting for you, and I want you. You'll win all the jackpots. Because I want you, I need you. Love me, I'm Maggie, I'm so alone, love me.

Kostner had been staring at the slot machine for a very long time, and his weary brown eyes had seemed to be locked to the blue eyes on the jackpot bars. But he knew no one else could see the blue eyes, and no one else could hear the voice, and no one else knew about Maggie. He was the universe to her. Everything to her.

He thumbed in another silver dollar, and the Pit Boss watched, the slot machine repairman watched, the Slot Machine Floor Manager watched, three change girls watched, and a pack of unidentified players watched, some from their seats.

The reels whirled, the handle snapped back, and in a second they flipped down to a halt, twenty silver dollars tokened themselves into the payoff trough and a woman at one of the crap tables belched a fragment of hysterical laughter.

And the gong went insane again.

The Floor Manager came over and said, very softly, "Mr. Kostner, it'll take us about fifteen minutes to pull this machine and check it out. I'm sure you understand." As two slot repairmen came out of the back, hauled the Chief off its stand, and took it into the repair room at the rear of the Casino.

While they waited, the Floor Manager regaled Kostner with stories of spooners who had used intricate magnets inside their clothes, of boomerang men who had attached their plastic implements under their sleeves so they could be extended on spring–loaded clips, of cheaters who had come equipped with tiny electric drills in their hands and wires that slipped into the tiny drilled holes. And he kept saying he knew Kostner would understand.

But Kostner knew the Floor Manager would not understand.

When they brought the Chief back, the repairmen nodded assuredly. "Nothing wrong with it. Works perfectly. Nobody's been boomin' it."

But the blue eyes were gone on the jackpot bars.

Kostner knew they would return.

They paid him off again.

He returned and played again. And again. And again. They put a "spotter" on him. He won again. And again. And again. The crowd had grown to massive proportions. Word had spread like the silent communications of the telegraph vine, up and down the Strip, all the way to downtown Vegas and the sidewalk casinos where they played night and day every day of the year, and the crowd moved toward the hotel, and the Casino, and the seedy–looking walker with his weary brown eyes. The crowd moved to him inexorably, drawn like lemmings by the odor of the luck that rose from him like musky electrical cracklings. And he won. Again and again. Thirty–eight thousand dollars. And the three blue eyes continued to stare up at him. Her lover was winning. Maggie and her Moneyeyes.

Finally, the Casino decided to speak to Kostner. They pulled the Chief for fifteen minutes, for a supplemental check by experts from the slot machine company in downtown Vegas, and while they were checking it, they asked Kostner to come to the main office of the hotel.

The owner was there. His face seemed faintly familiar to Kostner. Had he seen it on television? The newspapers?

"Mr. Kostner, my name is Jules Hartshorn."

"I'm pleased to meet you."

"Quite a string of luck you're having out there."

"It's been a long time coming."

"You realize, this sort of luck is impossible."

"I'm compelled to believe it, Mr. Hartshorn."

"Um. As am I. It's happening to my Casino. But we're thoroughly convinced of one of two possibilities, Mr. Kostner: one, either the machine is inoperable in a way we can't detect, or two, you are the cleverest spooner we've ever had in here."

"I'm not cheating."

"As you can see, Mr. Kostner, I'm smiling. The reason I'm smiling is at your naiveté in believing I would take your word for it. I'm perfectly happy to nod politely and say of course you aren't cheating. But no one can win thirty–eight thousand dollars on nineteen straight jackpots off one slot machine; it doesn't even have mathematical odds against its happening, Mr. Kostner. It's on a cosmic scale of improbability with three dark planets crashing into our sun within the next twenty minutes. It's on a par with the Pentagon, the Forbidden City and the

Kremlin all three pushing the red button at the same microsecond. It's an impossibility, Mr. Kostner. An impossibility that's happening to me."

"I'm sorry."

"Not really."

"No, not really. I can use the money."

"For what, exactly, Mr. Kostner?"

"I hadn't thought about it, really."

"I see. Well, Mr. Kostner, let's look at it this way. I can't stop you from playing, and if you continue to win, I'll be required to pay off. And no stubble–chinned thugs will be waiting in an alley to jackroll you and take the money. The checks will be honored. The best I can hope for, Mr. Kostner, is the attendant publicity. Right now, every player in Vegas is in that Casino, waiting for you to drop cartwheels into that machine. It won't make up for what I'm losing, if you continue the way you've been, but it will help. Every high–roller in town likes to rub up next to luck. All I ask is that you cooperate a little."

"The least I can do, considering your generosity."

"An attempt at humor."

"I'm sorry. What is it you'd like me to do?"

"Get about ten hours' sleep."

"While you pull the slot and have it worked over thoroughly?"

"Yes."

"If I wanted to keep winning, that might be a pretty stupid move on my part. You might change the thigamajig inside so I couldn't win if I put back every dollar of that thirty–eight grand."

"We're licensed by the state of Nevada, Mr. Kostner."

"I come from a good family, too, and take a look at me. I'm a bum with thirty–eight thousand dollars in my pocket."

"Nothing will be done to that slot machine, Kostner."

"Then why pull it for ten hours?"

"To work it over thoroughly in the shop. If something as undetectable as metal fatigue or a worn escalator tooth or—we want to make sure this doesn't happen with other machines. And the extra time will get the word around town; we can use the crowd. Some of those tourists will stick to our fingers, and it'll help defray the expense of having you break the bank at this Casino—on a slot machine."

"I have to take your word."

"This hotel will be in business long after you're gone, Kostner."

"Not if I keep winning."

Hartshorn's smile was a stricture. "A good point."

"So it isn't much of an argument."

"It's the only one I have. If you want to get back out on that floor, I can't stop you."

"No Mafia hoods ventilate me later?"

"I beg your pardon?"

"I said: no Maf—"

"You have a picturesque manner of speaking. In point of fact, I haven't the faintest idea what you're talking about."

"I'm sure you haven't."

"You've got to stop reading *The National Enquirer*. This is a legally run business. I'm merely asking a favor."

"Okay, Mr. Hartshorn, I've been three days without any sleep. Ten hours will do me a world of good."

"I'll have the desk clerk find you a quiet room on the top floor. And thank you, Mr. Kostner."

"Think nothing of it."

"I'm afraid that will be impossible."

"A lot of impossible things are happening lately."

He turned to go, as Hartshorn lit a cigarette.

"Oh, by the way, Mr. Kostner?"

Kostner stopped and half–turned. "Yes?"

His eyes were getting difficult to focus. There was a ringing in his ears. Hartshorn seemed to waver at the edge of his vision like heat lightning across a prairie. Like memories of things Kostner had come across the country to forget. Like the whimpering and pleading that kept tugging at the cells of his brain. The voice of Maggie. Still back in there, saying . . . things . . .

They'll try to keep you from me.

All he could think about was the ten hours of sleep he had been promised. Suddenly it was more important than the money, than forgetting, than anything. Hartshorn was talking, was saying things, but Kostner could not hear him. It was as if he had turned off the sound and saw only the silent rubbery movement of Hartshorn's lips. He shook his head trying to clear it.

There were half a dozen Hartshorns all melting into and out of one another. And the voice of Maggie.

I'm warm here, and alone. I could be good to you, if you can come to me. Please come, please hurry.

"Mr. Kostner?"

Hartshorn's voice came draining down through silt as thick as velvet flocking. Kostner tried to focus again. His extremely weary brown eyes began to track.

"Did you know about that slot machine?" Hartshorn was saying. "A peculiar thing happened with it about six weeks ago."

"What was that?"

"A girl died playing it. She had a heart attack, a seizure while she was pulling the handle, and died right out there on the floor."

Kostner was silent for a moment. He wanted desperately to ask Hartshorn what color the dead girl's eyes had been, but he was afraid the owner would say blue.

He paused with his hand on the office door. "Seems as though you've had nothing but a streak of bad luck on that machine."

Hartshorn smiled an enigmatic smile. "It might not change for a while, either."

Kostner felt his jaw muscles tighten. "Meaning I might die, too, and wouldn't *that* be bad luck."

Hartshorn's smile became hieroglyphic, permanent, stamped on him forever. "Sleep tight, Mr. Kostner."

In a dream, she came to him. Long, smooth thighs and soft golden down on her arms; blue eyes deep as the past, misted with a fine scintillance like lavender spiderwebs; taut body that was the only body Woman had ever had, from the very first. Maggie came to him.

Hello, I've been traveling a long time.

"Who are you?" Kostner asked, wonderingly. He was standing on a chilly plain, or was it a plateau? The wind curled around them both, or was it only around him? She was exquisite, and he saw her clearly, or was it through a mist? Her voice was deep and resonant, or was it light and warm as night–blooming jasmine?

I'm Maggie. I love you. I've waited for you.

"You have blue eyes."

Yes. *With love.*

"You're very beautiful."

Thank you. *With female amusement.*

"But why me? Why let it happen to me? Are you the girl who—are you the one that was sick—the one who—?"

I'm Maggie. And you, I picked you, because you need me. You've needed someone for a long long time.

Then it unrolled for Kostner. The past unrolled and he saw who he was. He saw himself alone. Always alone. As a child, born to kind and warm parents who hadn't the vaguest notion of who he was, what he wanted to be, where his talents lay. So he had run off, when he was in his teens, and alone always alone on the road. For years and months and days and hours, with no one. Casual friendships, based on food, or sex, or artificial similarities. But no one to whom he could cleave, and cling, and belong. It was that way till Susie, and with her he had found light. He had discovered the scents and aromas of a spring that was eternally one day away. He had laughed, really laughed, and known with her it would at last be all right. So he had poured all of himself into her, giving her everything; all his hopes, his secret thoughts, his tender dreams; and she had taken them, taken him, all of him, and he had known for the first time what it was to have a place to live, to have a home in someone's heart. It was all the silly and gentle things he laughed at in other people, but for him it was breathing deeply of wonder.

He had stayed with her for a long time, and had supported her, supported her son from the first marriage; the marriage Susie never talked about. And then one day, he had come back, as Susie had always known he would. He was a dark creature of ruthless habits and vicious nature, but she had been his woman, all along, and Kostner realized he had been used as a stop–gap, as a bill–payer till her wandering terror came home to nest. Then she had asked him to leave. Broke, and tapped out in all the silent inner ways a man can be drained, he had left, without even a fight, for all the fight had been leeched out of him. He had left, and wandered West, and finally come to Las Vegas, where he had hit bottom. And found Maggie. In a dream, with blue eyes, he had found Maggie.

I want you to belong to me. I love you. *Her truth was vibrant in Kostner's mind. She was his, at last someone who was special, was his.*

"Can I trust you? I've never been able to trust anyone before. Women, never. But I need someone. I really need someone."

It's me, always. Forever. You can trust me.

And she came to him, fully. Her body was a declaration of truth and trust such as no other Kostner had ever known before. She met him on a windswept plain of thought, and he made love to her more completely than he had known

147

any passion before. She joined with him, entered him, mingled with his blood and his thought and his frustration, and he came away clean, filled with glory.

"Yes, I can trust you, I want you, I'm yours," he whispered to her, when they lay side by side in a dream nowhere Of mist and soundlessness. "I'm yours."

She smiled, a woman's smile of belief in her man; a smile of trust and deliverance. And Kostner woke up.

The Chief was back on its stand, and the crowd had been penned back by velvet ropes. Several people had played the machine, but there had been no jackpots.

Now Kostner came into the Casino, and the "spotters" got themselves ready. While Kostner had slept, they had gone through his clothes, searching for wires, for gaffs, for spoons or boomerangs. Nothing.

Now he walked straight to the Chief, and stared at it.

Hartshorn was there. "You look tired," he said gently to Kostner, studying the man's weary brown eyes.

"I am, a little," Kostner tried a smile, which didn't work. "I had a funny dream."

"Oh?"

"Yeah . . . about a girl . . . " He let it die off.

Hartshorn's smile was understanding. Pitying, empathic and understanding. "There are lots of girls in this town. You shouldn't have any trouble finding one with your winnings."

Kostner nodded, and slipped his first silver dollar into the slot. He pulled the handle. The reels spun with a ferocity Kostner had not heard before and suddenly everything went whipping slant–wise as he felt a wrenching of pure flame in his stomach, as his head was snapped on its spindly neck, as the lining behind his eyes was burned out. There was a terrible shriek, of tortured metal, of an express train ripping the air with its passage, of a hundred small animals being gutted and torn to shreds, of incredible pain, of night winds that tore the tops off mountains of lava. And a keening whine of a voice that wailed and wailed and wailed as it went away from there in blinding light —

Free! Free! Heaven or Hell it doesn't matter! Free!

The sound of a soul released from an eternal prison, a genie freed from a dark bottle. And in that instant of damp soundless nothingness, Kostner saw the reels snap and clock down for the final time:

One, two, three. Blue eyes.

But he would never cash his checks.

The crowd screamed through one voice as he fell sidewise and lay on his face. The final loneliness . . .

The Chief was pulled. Bad luck. Too many gamblers resented its very presence in the Casino. So it was pulled. And returned to the company, with explicit instructions it was to be melted down to slag. And not till it was in the hands of the ladle foreman, who was ready to dump it into the slag furnace, did anyone remark on the final tally the Chief had clocked.

"Look at that, ain't that weird," said the ladle foreman to his bucket man. He pointed to the three glass windows.

"Never saw jackpot bars like that before," the bucket man agreed. "Three eyes. Must be an old machine."

"Yeah, some of these old games go way back," the foreman said, hoisting the slot machine onto the conveyor track leading to the slag furnace.

"Three eyes, huh. How about that. Three brown eyes." And he threw the knife–switch that sent the Chief down the track, to puddle in the roaring inferno of the furnace.

Three brown *eyes.*

Three brown eyes that looked very very weary. That looked very very trapped. That looked very very betrayed. Some of these old games go way back.

Biography

Harlan Ellison®

Harlan Ellison® was recently characterized by *The New York Times Book Review* as having "the spellbinding quality of a great nonstop talker, with a cultural warehouse for a mind." *The Los Angeles Times* suggested, "It's long past time for Harlan Ellison to be awarded the title: 20th century Lewis Carroll." And the *Washington Post Book World* said simply, "One of the great living American short story writers."

He has written or edited 76 books; more than 1,700 short stories, essay, articles, and newspaper columns; two dozen teleplays, for which he received the Writers Guild of America most outstanding teleplay award for solo work an unprecedented *four* times; and a dozen movies. Currently a member of the Writers Guild of America, he has twice served on the board of the WGAW. He won the Mystery Writers of America Edgar Allan Poe award twice, the Horror Writers Association Bram Stoker award six times (including the Lifetime Achievement Award in 1996), the Nebula award of the Science Fiction Writers of America three times, the Hugo (World Science Fiction Convention achievement award) 8-1/2 times, and received the Silver Pen for Journalism from P.E.N. Not to mention the World Fantasy Award; the British Fantasy Award; the American Mystery Award; plus two Audie Awards and a Grammy nomination for Spoken Word recordings.

He created great fantasies for the 1985 CBS revival of *The Twilight Zone* (including Danny Kaye's final performance) and *The Outer Limits*; travelled with The Rolling Stones; marched with Martin Luther King from Selma to Montgomery; created roles for Buster Keaton, Wally Cox, Gloria Swanson and nearly 100 other stars on *Burke's Law*; ran with a kid gang in Brooklyn's Red Hook to get background for his first novel; covered race riots in Chicago's "back of the yards" with the late James Baldwin; sang with, and dined with, Maurice Chevalier; once stood off the son of a Detroit Mafia kingpin with a Remington XP-100 pistol-rifle while wearing nothing but a bath towel; sued Paramount and ABC-TV for plagiarism and won $337,000. His most recent legal victory, in protection of copyright against global Internet piracy of writers' work, in May of 2004—a 4-year-long litigation against AOL et al.—has resulted in revolutionizing protection of creative properties on the Web. (As promised, he has repaid hundreds of contributions [totaling $50,000] from the KICK Internet Piracy support fund.) But the bottom line, as voiced by *Booklist* in 2008, is this: "One thing for sure: the man can write."

And, as Tom Snyder said on the CBS *Late, Late Show*: "An amazing talent; meeting him is an incredible experience." He was a regular on ABC-TV's *Politically Incorrect* with Bill Maher.

In 1990, Ellison was honored by P.E.N. for his continuing commitment to artistic freedom and the battle against censorship, "In defense of the First Amendment."

Harlan Ellison's 1992 novelette "The Man Who Rowed Christopher Columbus Ashore" was selected from more than 6,000 short stories published in the U.S. for inclusion in the 1993 edition of *The Best American Short Stories*.

Mr. Ellison worked as a creative consultant and host for *2000ˣ*, a series of 26 one-hour dramatized radio adaptations of famous SF stories for The Hollywood Theater of the Ear; and for his work was presented with the prestigious Ray Bradbury Award for Drama Series. The series was broadcast on National Public Radio in 2000 and 2001. Ellison's classic story "'Repent, Harlequin!' Said the Ticktockman" was included as part of this significant series, starring Robin Williams and the author in the title roles.

On June 22, 2002, at the 4th World Skeptics Convention, Harlan Ellison was presented with the *Distinguished Skeptic Award* by The Committee for the Scientific Investigation of the Paranormal (CSICOP) "in recognition of his outstanding contributions to the defense of science and critical thinking."

To celebrate the golden anniversary of Harlan Ellison's half century of storytelling, Morpheus International, publishers of *The Essential Ellison: A 35-Year Retrospective*, commissioned the book's primary editor, award-winning Australian writer and critic Terry Dowling, to expand Ellison's three-and-a-half decade collection into a 50-year retrospective. Mr. Dowling went through fifteen years of new stories and essays to pick what he thought were the most representative to be included in this 1000+ page collection. Along with *The Essential Ellison: A 50-Year Retrospective* (Morpheus International), Mr. Ellison's first Young Adult collection, *Troublemakers* is currently available in bookstores.

Among his most recognized works, translated into more than 40 languages and selling in the millions of copies, are *Deathbird Stories, Strange Wine, Approaching Oblivion, I Have No Mouth, & I Must Scream, Web of the City, Angry Candy, Love Ain't Nothing But Sex Misspelled, Ellison Wonderland, Memos From Purgatory, All The Lies That Are My Life, Shatterday, Mind Fields, An Edge In My Voice, Slippage* and *Stalking the Nightmare*. As creative intelligence and editor of the all-time best-selling *Dangerous Visions* anthologies and *Medea: Harlan's World*, he has been awarded two Special Hugos and the prestigious academic Milford Award for Lifetime Acheivement in Editing. In 2006, Harlan Ellison was named the Grand Master of the Science Fiction/Fantasy Writers of America.

In October 2002, Edgeworks Abbey and iBooks published the 35th Anniversary Edition of the highly acclaimed anthology *Dangerous Visions*.

In the November 2002 issue of *PC Gamer*, Ellison's hands-on creation of the CD-Rom game *I Have No Mouth, and I Must Scream*, based on the award-winning story of the same name, was voted "One of the 10 scariest PC games ever." ("I Have No Mouth, and I Must Scream" is one of the ten most reprinted stories in the English language.)

June 2003: A new Edition of *Vic & Blood*, published by iBooks in association with Edgeworks Abbey, collected for the first time both the complete graphic novel cycle *and* Ellison's stories including the 1969 novella favorite from which the legendary cult film *A Boy and His Dog* was made.

December 2003: Ellison edited a collection of Edwardian mystery-puzzle stories titled *Jacques Futrelle's "The Thinking Machine*, published by The Modern Library.

October 2004: A new edition of *Strange Wine*, published by iBooks in association with Edgeworks Abbey.

May 2006: Ellison and Oscar nominee Josh Olson (for his adaptation of *A History of Violence*) collaborated on a teleplay "The Discarded" (based on Ellison's short story of the same name) for the ABC television series *Masters of Science Fiction*.

November 2006: A new edition of *Spider Kiss*, published by M Press, in association with Edgeworks Abbey. The second book in the M Press / Edgeworks Abbey series, *Harlan Ellison's Watching*, was released in a new edition in 2008.

March 2007: Based on Ellison's work, *Harlan Ellison's Dream Corridor (Volume Two)* is released. Ellison introduces a dozen tales in this new collection, featuring adaptations of some of his greatest stories by some of the most respected names in comics, including Neal Adams, Gene Colan, Richard Corben, Paul Chadwick...and the very last work by the late, great *Superman* artist, Curt Swan.

April 2007: A special world premiere screening is held of *Dreams With Sharp Teeth*. For more than twenty-five years, documentarian Erik Nelson (*Grizzly Man*) has been interviewing Ellison and friends [including Josh Olson (*A History of Violence*), Neil Gaiman (*Anansi Boys*, Dan Simmons (*The Terror*), Peter David (*Fallen Angel*), Michael Cassutt (*Tango Midnight*), Ron Moore (*Battlestar Galactica*), and actor Robin Williams] to produce a feature-length look at the life and work of Harlan Ellison: *Dreams With Sharp Teeth*. In 2008, the documentary was featured at The South by Southwest Conference and Festival, The Edinburgh Film Festival, The Independent Festival in Boston and opened at both the prestigious Lincoln Center in New York and The NY Film Forum. In celebration of his 75th birthday, *Dreams With Sharp Teeth* will premiere on the Sundance Film Channel and be released on DVD in May 2009.

Harlan Ellison lives with his wife, Susan, inside The Lost Aztec Temple of Mars, in Los Angeles.

OPEN ROAD

INTEGRATED MEDIA

Open Road Integrated Media is a digital publisher and multimedia content company. Open Road creates connections between authors and their audiences by marketing its ebooks through a new proprietary online platform, which uses premium video content and social media.

Videos, Archival Documents, and New Releases

Sign up for the Open Road Media newsletter and get news delivered straight to your inbox.

Sign up now at
www.openroadmedia.com/newsletters

FIND OUT MORE AT
WWW.OPENROADMEDIA.COM

FOLLOW US:
@openroadmedia and
Facebook.com/OpenRoadMedia

CPSIA information can be obtained
at www.ICGtesting.com
Printed in the USA
BVOW08s2315040917
493739BV00002B/2/P